SAILING
FREEDOM

Martha Bennett Stiles

SQUARE
FISH

Henry Holt and Company
New York

For my great-nephew Raymond Justin Robins,
whose father and grandfather and great-grandfather
went down to the sea in ships

SQUARE
FISH

An Imprint of Macmillan
175 Fifth Avenue, New York, NY 10010
mackids.com

SAILING TO FREEDOM. Text copyright © 2012 by Martha Bennett Stiles.
All rights reserved. Printed in the United States of America by
R. R. Donnelley & Sons Company, Harrisonburg, Virginia.

Square Fish and the Square Fish logo are trademarks of Macmillan and
are used by Henry Holt and Company under license from Macmillan.

Square Fish books may be purchased for business or promotional use. For information
on bulk purchases, please contact the Macmillan Corporate and Premium Sales
Department at (800) 221-7945 x 5442 or by e-mail at specialmarkets@macmillan.com.

Library of Congress Cataloging-in-Publication Data
Stiles, Martha Bennett.
Sailing to freedom / Martha Bennett Stiles.
p.   cm.
Summary: In the mid-eighteen hundreds, while serving as cook's apprentice on his
uncle's schooner with his pet monkey, Allie, twelve-year-old Ray discovers that they
are transporting a fugitive slave to the free north.
ISBN 978-1-250-03991-0 (paperback) / ISBN 978-1-4668-2578-9 (e-book)
[1. Fugitive slaves—Fiction. 2. Slavery—Fiction. 3. Boats and
boating—Fiction. 4. Capuchin monkeys—Fiction. 5. Monkeys as
pets—Fiction. 6. Uncles—Fiction. 7. United States—History—
1849–1877—Fiction.] I. Title.
PZ7.S8557Sai 2012   [Fic]—dc23   2011025589

Originally published in the United States by Henry Holt and Company
First Square Fish Edition: 2014
Book designed by Elynn Cohen
Square Fish logo designed by Filomena Tuosto

1 3 5 7 9 10 8 6 4 2

AR: 5.7 / LEXILE: 890L

CONTENTS

Chapter 1

A Sudden Journey

D r. Spofford delivered me, Raymond Justin Ingle, Jr., into the town of Newburyport, Massachusetts, the very day that the Spanish slave ship *Amistad* wound up at Long Island in August of 1839. So if you've got two hands and a foot, you can calculate that I turned twelve last summer— and twelve is *plenty* old enough to go to sea. This May, Father's clipper ship, the *Black Skimmer*, was booked to take a shipload of South Carolina cotton to Liverpool, England. Father'd been home less than three weeks when he had to leave Mam and me again. One more time, I begged him to let me sail with him.

Allie, the black-and-white capuchin monkey who'd ridden Father's shoulder right into the house this homecoming, stared down at me with what I took for sympathy, but Father laughed. "Not till the top of your head reaches the bottom of the mantelpiece, Ray." He laughed again when I pushed my fingers upward through my hair and ran to the fireplace. Mam followed close.

Not a hair touched wood. Mam looked glad.

In the short time Father'd been home, I'd developed a liking for Allie, but now I glared at her. No more full-grown than I, but *she* was a veteran sailor. "I don't want to be tall!" I cried. "Tall people bump their stupid heads!" Then I swallowed. Father's the tallest one in his family, taller than both his brothers.

Mam's firm ambition is to teach me not to blurt things without thinking. I waited for the ceiling to fall on me—or at least the mantelpiece. Father just said, "One of these days, Ray, you'll be able to lift that mantel right off its supports with that hard head of yours. Time enough to talk about climbing the rigging."

So much for Mam telling me "it's not how tall you *are*; it's how tall you *act*."

Singing "The Sailor's Alphabet" is how Mam taught me my letters. Father taught me to tie shoelaces and masthead knots the same week. Then he sailed for Manila. I swore someday I'd sail with him.

"Dr. Spofford says sea air makes you grow."

Father ruffled my hair, which you cannot do to anybody near as tall as you are, and which I hate. "*Time* makes you grow," he said. "Cheer up, Ray. Look at your feet. Remember when ol' Matt was a pup, how funny his big feet looked under that scrawny body? And everybody said, 'He'll surely be a big dog; see his big feet'?"

Matthew G. Perry was a stray pup our minister harbored, scrawny because he had worms. With the whole Belleville Church congregation slipping him treats, he got big as a billy goat soon enough. I don't have worms the way Matt did, but I'm skinny and short anyway.

But yes, big feet. Which Father seems to think is a hopeful sign.

Then Father got serious. "Son, the sailor who sold me this monkey loved her, and I hope you will too." Out of the side of my eye, I saw Mam stiffen, so I wasn't the only one surprised.

"She needs a lot of understanding," Father went on. Mam pursed her lips. I started being careful to look only at Father and his little monkey. "First she was taken from her mother." Allie's black eyes got so big, anybody would've thought she understood Father's words. "Then whoever committed that crime sold her to a sailor. Now that sailor's father's died, and the sailor has to quit the sea and run the farm for his mother—and his mother won't let a monkey in her house." Father gave Mam his warmest smile. Obviously she'd let that monkey in *her* house. But he didn't seem to have warned her he was going to leave Allie with me! My arms and legs tingled.

Father's always given me good-bye presents, as if a present could make up for being left behind. Never anything like Allie, though. I could hardly nerve myself to sneak a look at Mam, but when I did, my chest filled up so hard it hurt my backbone. Mam can never say no to Father when he's about to sail. Allie was mine.

In my pocket I had a half-eaten apple. I held it up to her. She looked at me as carefully as she looked at the apple, then snatched it as if she feared I'd change my mind.

"Good thinking," said Father as Allie chewed in his ear. "I knew I was leaving her in good hands."

I leaned my head sideways so Father could set Allie on my shoulder. She felt warm against my neck. Her fur had an outdoors smell, kind of like my friend Tom Chase's cat, which spends every night hunting. Her small hand holding tight to a hank of my hair felt as if she trusted me, a good feeling. And now that she was going to have to stay in Newburyport too, I didn't feel jealous of her anymore.

In school, we're reminded every May 10 that it's the anniversary of going to war with the Barbary pirates. Nobody's ever going to have to remind me that May 10 is the anniversary of when I got Allie.

Nice as keeping Allie was, in the weeks after Father left, I couldn't help complaining. Having

Allie *and* sailing with Father would've been a whole lot nicer.

Ever since Dr. Spofford told Mam I'm the only child she's ever going to have, Mam's been even surer than Father that I'm too short for sea duty. "What am I always telling you when you fuss?" she demanded.

"Be-as-patient-as-the-*Amistad*ers," we recited in unison. Nearly three years passed after those men took over their captors' ship before they got back to Africa.

"Mam's big on recommending patience," I groused to Allie. "Like when we had to stand on the dock with her, watching the *Black Skimmer* disappear. 'Patience, patience,' she said. Remember?"

Patience, Mam says when the gingerbread in the oven smells so good it's surely got to be ready to eat, whatever the cookbook says.

Patience, she says when that lunk Clam Hopkins calls me Shrimp. (True, if I don't patiently wait to punch him till school's out, I get caned.)

Patience, she says when our minister's wife pinches my cheek and urges me to be *a Ray of sunshine, a Ray of hope*. Mostly I'm proud to be

Raymond Justin Ingle, Jr., but some aching-cheek Sundays, I secretly wish I were Uncle Thad's name-sake instead of Father's.

"If you ever get a chance," I instructed Allie, "I'd like you to bite that hand reaching for my cheek." But *no taking a monkey to church* was another thing Mam stayed firm about, Sunday after Sunday.

Mam was firm, and Allie and I had to be patient, when come June, Mam got a letter from her sister in Boston. "Doctor says this baby I'm carrying is twins!" Aunt Lou wrote. "Says I must lie abed till they come because—" There Mam stopped reading aloud, and for a moment all I heard was Great-grandfather's tall clock ticking. Then, "Wash your face and pack, Ray." Mam was halfway across the parlor, headed for the stairs.

"Are we going to Boston?"

"*I'm* going to Boston. You're going to your uncle's."

"Oh no," I moaned. "There's got to be some-where else I could go!"

"You, yes," Mam answered over her shoulder. "You and Allie?"

Slowly Allie and I followed Mam upstairs. I have two uncles, but only one lives in Newburyport, so I knew which uncle Mam meant. Some summer vacation. Old skinny-as-a-garter-snake Uncle Slye, such a miser he's stingy even with himself, would be worse than school.

I checked my face in my glass. Father's cowlick; Mam's brown hair and eyes; a nose beginning to lengthen, I think; one small forehead scar; one streak. I spat on my shirttail, swiped at the streak. "Father has two older brothers," I told Allie as I packed. "Uncle Thad lives on the *Newburyport Beauty,* his own schooner. He's probably somewhere between Salem and Rockport right now. Uncle Slye lives just a few blocks downhill from here at Ingle's, his grocery store.

"Uncle Thad has three daughters in Rockport. When I tell you I'd rather we were going to stay with three girl cousins than with Uncle Slye, you'll start to get an idea what we're in for. The only time Uncle Slye smiles is when somebody overpays him by mistake."

Uncle Thad's one son died of flu. I didn't mention that to Allie. She wasn't listening anyhow.

Too busy spitting on her paw and rubbing her cheek. The way Allie imitates, I guess I should stop wishing she could talk. I'm always saying something I wish I hadn't!

Mam and I had flu the same time as my cousin. Mam lost the baby she was carrying, and Dr. Spofford told her there wouldn't ever be another. Since then, she's made sure that Father keeps in mind how short I am.

While Mam and I were sick, Father hired a woman named Cora from Guinea, the neighborhood where all Newburyport's black people live, to take care of us. Cora's husband is the cook on Uncle Thad's schooner. He and Cora used to live in South Carolina, she told me. She said the Underground Railroad had helped her husband get from South Carolina to Newburyport, and that later, as soon as he could, he'd sent for her. Now her husband works for Uncle Thad. I tried to get Cora to tell me about the Underground Railroad, about how they'd helped her husband, but she just said, "Crowd your brain with what you don't need to know, you might find you ain't got room left for what you better had know!"

Instead she told me stories about Buh Rabbit, a critter who's a lot shorter than his enemy, Buh Wolf, but always beats him. For a long time I used to wish I could be sick again so I could hear more of Cora's stories. Back then, my favorite was the one where Buh Rabbit begs Buh Wolf to throw him in the fire instead of the briar patch. Now I'd like to get her to tell Allie and me one with a monkey in it.

Father says capuchins don't come from Africa, though, and Allie and I'd want a story about a monkey that looks like her. She has snow white fur all around her face and neck, and her face is as pink as Tom Chase's baby sister. (Mam swears that ruff makes Allie look like Queen Elizabeth, calls her Your Highness often as not.) Allie's tail is as long as Matthew G. Perry's, though he was ten times bigger than she is even before Belleville's congregation started slipping him treats. Walking to the post office with her on my shoulder turns heads. And that's as good as a story.

I tried to weigh Allie on Mam's kitchen scales while Mam was gardening, but Allie wouldn't hold still. I calculate she weighs about two pounds. Like me, she's still growing. (I hope like me, anyway.) For now, she rides everywhere on my shoulder and never makes it ache.

On my shoulder is where Allie perched when Mam marched us to Uncle Slye's store. We made better time than I liked. From our house on High Street to Ingle's Groceries on State is downhill more ways than one.

I opened the door to Ingle's for Mam. *Clang* went its bell. "Uncle Slye's quarters are behind the store," I'd told Allie before we set out. "If a customer comes when he's there, he wants to hustle back in. Somebody might snitch something! Uncle Slye doesn't have a door between his rooms and the shop, just a curtain, so he can hear that bell."

Uncle Slye wears rimless glasses and smells like old paper. He's so pale from sitting inside reading his ledger, his face reminds me of the greenish color my cousin's marble gravestone turns in the leaf-filtered sunshine. Out from behind his counter he stepped, smiling like a crocodile, until he realized Mam hadn't come to shop. "Here? A growing boy?

He'll eat me out of stock! I'll be turning away *customers!*" He glared at Allie. "And what does *that* godless critter eat?"

"Just scraps," I answered quickly, giving Allie's foot a squeeze so she'd know I didn't mean it.

"Ray will help in your store to pay for his keep." Mam stuck out her chin. To keep Uncle Slye from arguing, or to keep me from protesting? Either way, it worked.

I wondered how long Mam's chin would affect Uncle Slye after she took it to Boston and left me and Allie alone with him.

She didn't embarrass me by hugging me good-bye in front of Uncle Slye. (Mam grew up with brothers.) She just squeezed my shoulder hard and told me she wouldn't be gone any longer than she had to be.

"Tie that varmint to a loft post!" Uncle Slye ordered the minute she was gone.

I was afraid the dark loft would scare Allie. She could hurt herself trying to get loose.

"She could earn money for you down here," I suggested.

Uncle Slye's whole body came to attention.

"How about a sign on the counter, 'Feed the Monkey a Peanut, One Copper'?"

Uncle Slye prints very clearly.

I set Allie on a cracker barrel beside the counter and told her, "Stay put!" She got her serious expression. I couldn't tell what she was thinking. I could guess what Uncle Slye was thinking, but he just went around the counter to sit on his own stool and told me to get a rag and polish the front window.

I was glad to be interrupted by a customer, until he handed me a paper bag and said, "Fill this with molasses, boy."

Cheap molasses that hasn't had all the water boiled out will soak through paper. I held that sack at arm's length under cheap Uncle Slye's molasses barrel spigot. Was I relieved when the sack held! The man started to pay me, but Uncle Slye was right there to take the money.

Our next visitor ordered "two pickles, boy."

Every dry day since Father'd sailed without me again, I'd been hooking my feet over a branch in our yard, then hanging as long as I could, trying to stretch myself taller. Allie would wrap her tail around the same branch and hang beside me. Now as I rolled up my sleeve, I wished I'd hung by my hands some too. My arm was in moldy brine to my elbow before I reached pickles.

Nobody'd fallen for our peanuts sign, but at least Allie stayed where I'd set her, watching everything. I had the feeling that by evening she'd be able to do anything I'd done.

At noon, three different sets of church bells rang twelve. Each started four beats after the other, like round singers. (Newburyporters set their clocks depending on which church they go to.) I looked hopefully at Uncle Slye, but he seemed to be playing deaf. Finally at one o'clock, he went into his quarters and fetched me a plate of cold boiled salt buffalo tongue.

"I'm not dining with that varmint!" he declared, and stamped back behind his curtain.

I sat on Uncle Slye's stool, and Allie perched on my shoulder so I could hand her up bits of tongue. We hadn't swallowed three bites before we began to smell frying onions.

Midafternoon I was bagging peppermints, and Uncle Slye was watching to make sure I didn't pop one in my mouth, when my classmates Tom Chase and Clam Hopkins walked in. I hadn't shown up for baseball, so they'd tracked me down. Clam smirked at my apron, but Tom said, "I'm aiming to take the sloop out, Ray. Come along?"

Uncle Slye inhaled.

"Not today," I answered Tom, loud and clear. "Buy some peanuts," I whispered. "I'll pay you back."

Clam pretended not to hear, but Tom fed Allie three peanuts and left. Tom knows about chores. The Chases have two goats, and we can never go sailing till they're milked. You can bet I help!

Clam's never helped anybody. That scar on my forehead is where Clam got me with a snowball he claimed he didn't know had gravel in it.

"It's your own fault, for calling him Clam," Mam said.

"Nobody but his mother's called him Andrew since the day he admitted to *liking* clam chowder," I told her. "Ugh."

"Well," she said, "if you can't learn manners or kindness, you'll have to learn to dodge."

Clam *is* a funny nickname for somebody whose

mouth is never shut. In the cartoons Tom Chase draws on his slate, "Andrew" is always a clam with bubbles rising from its wide-open shell.

One day after baseball, when everybody'd come to my house for lemonade and Clam was talking as usual, he came out with, "If you ask me, those Bostonians ought to run every abolitionist out of town!"

"Well, then, I hope the abolitionists all run to Newburyport!" I said, thinking of how Cora'd said they'd helped her husband.

Mam gave me the look she gets when telling me not to shoot off my mouth half-cocked. "Remember, Ray," she lectured me at supper, "a fly doesn't enter a shut mouth."

It was all Allie and I could do *not* to keep our mouths shut come suppertime at Uncle Slye's. He did fix something better than cold tongue: fried sausage. Only all Allie and I got of it was its smell through the loft floorboards. For us it was tongue again, and once we'd eaten as much of it as we could stomach, Uncle Slye'd sent us up for the night with one quilt and a chamber pot.

The loft was hot enough to smoke ham, so I just

lay on top of the quilt. Soon Allie was snoring softly, like the waves lapping at Plum Island's shore. Lying on that hard floor, I dreamt I was chained in the hold of the *Amistad* with those slaves.

Allie didn't have any problem. She slept on my stomach.

But when the sunrise bells woke me, she was gone.

She'd seemed so afraid of Uncle Slye, I'd never imagined she'd leave my side. I grabbed my trousers, didn't stop for shoes or shirt. I *had* to find Allie before Uncle Slye woke up!

Low Country, South Carolina, April 1852

I t hadn't been the new baby's cries in the room below that had wakened Ogun in his loft bunk, but that rare thing, his mother's voice rising. Ogun had slid out from under his blanket, crawled as soundlessly as possible across the splintery boards to the ladder hole, and lain there shivering, listening.

"Cold water to my middle all day," he'd heard his father say. "Hoeing another man's rice! Buckra rice! No more!"

Lying there with a cramp in his leg, Ogun had turned first hot with shock and baffled anger, then cold with misery. His father was leaving.

Ogun would be eleven in two days. Always before on his birthday his father had taken him fishing at the workday's end. Always. Where was he going? "Surely," Ogun thought, "if he cared about me, he could wait three days to go there." But the door had opened, and the door had closed.

Ogun can't remember the grandfather who was sent by the overseer to Charleston to buy nails and never came back. ("They find he boat upside down in the water," his mother tells him.) Ogun wouldn't know his grandfather if the two of them shared an oar, but he remembers his beloved grandmother, Nana Cora, well. He misses her Buh Rabbit stories. Big as he is, he misses her lap. And now his father?

Ogun is too old to throw his arms around his mother and beg her not to leave him, forbid her to leave him, but he watches her. When he can, he watches her, but she is not part of any work crew again yet. That baby—as Ogun thinks of his little sister—that baby is still too new. All day as he carries water to the corn planters, Ogun wonders, his stomach tight, if he will find his mother in the cabin at the workday's end.

Chapter 2

A Soft Answer Turneth Away Wrath

A terrible sight greeted me. Allie *did* know how to do everything she'd seen me do! But she wasn't interested in weighing sugar or polishing glass. She was interested in that molasses spigot. She was interested in the bushel baskets of peanuts sitting right on the floor. Her wicked pink face was smeared with molasses from chin to nostrils, and in a voice pitched high with excitement, she urged me to join the fun.

I snatched her up, sticky as she was. Her chatter got even shriller. Taking the stairs two at a time, I was halfway aloft when I heard Uncle Slye howl. I glanced over my shoulder but kept moving. Uncle Slye's bald spot was red as a tomato. He'd heard Allie and, still in his nightshirt, hurried into the shop.

On the shop floor was a spreading pool of molasses with about half a bushel of unshelled peanuts and hulls mixed in. Allie'd first eaten all she wanted, I guess, then begun to play. Uncle Slye's screams were something between a steamboat whistle and a stuck pig.

In the loft, I snatched up yesterday's shirt, knotted one of its arms around Allie's waist and the other around a post. She just hunkered down and started licking molasses off her knees.

I didn't pause to try to clean mine. Sticky as Buh Rabbit after he met the Tar Baby, I hurried down to face Uncle Slye.

Uncle Slye commenced yelling at me before I left the stairs. "Look what you've done, bringing that demon into my store! That's a month's profits, that's—"

A soft answer turneth away wrath, Mam reminds me, but what I blurted to Uncle Slye was, "Well, it's your fault Allie woke up hungry! So did I!"

Uncle Slye was so mad he was shaking. "Do you know what it costs to feed a boy, just one day? Just one meal? I'm a plain storekeeper. I can't afford to stuff every relative whose ma wants a vacation! Let alone their menageries!"

"Father *said* you were always mean!" I yelled right back. "Said you'd eat a *bag* of candy one piece at a time right in front of him and Uncle Thad, never give either one of 'em a single lick! Said he and Uncle Thad could've caught a weasel asleep as easy as ever shared your toffee!"

For a freezing instant, Uncle Slye just stared at me. Then he hissed, "Get this floor clean. And get that animal out of my store before sundown or I'll *strangle* her!"

Too late, I didn't speak a word.

An empty leather water bucket stays near Ingle's front door, in case of fire. Two more, full of sand, stand beside it. I fetched one of those.

It was no heavier than my heart.

With Allie, I didn't miss my parents so much.

Now I was going to miss them *and* Allie. And in Allie's case, it would be forever.

I poured sand over the molasses. Then I fetched the empty water bucket and Uncle Slye's hearth shovel and began scraping the mixture up into both buckets. Uncle Slye went back to his room— to dress and eat his breakfast, I guess. He didn't say anything about mine.

As for Allie's, judging by the number of hulls I was shoveling, she'd eaten enough to stuff an elephant.

I scraped up as much of our joint creation as I could and lugged the buckets out to empty them under the lilac bush beside Uncle Slye's pump. I hurried, dreading to hear screams from the loft. Allie's teeth are sharp; nobody was going to strangle her, but if Uncle Slye took his ax . . .

I couldn't part with Allie.

Could the two of us hide on Plum Island till Mam came home? Live on fish? Between the lighthouse keeper and picnickers, not a chance.

How many times has Father said, "An *old* fish, Ray, is a fish that's known how to keep its mouth shut." I didn't know which I hated worse, Uncle Slye or my big yap.

I filled the buckets with water, took them inside, fetched a mop. Even over the sour, smoky, spilled-molasses odor, I could smell bacon frying behind Uncle Slye's curtain. My stomach yowled. Keeping my eye on that curtain, I stuck a hand into a sack of molasses flippers ("one copper each") on the bottom shelf behind the counter. Weary of the smell of molasses as I was, I found those big soft cakes so satisfying, I risked sneaking three before I'd finished mopping. Finally I made my last trip to the lilacs. When Uncle Slye returned from his breakfast, I was going to have to ask him where he got sand. Meanwhile the buckets that I returned to their places weren't any emptier than I felt. My breakfast sat on the counter: cold porridge. I plunked right down on the floor behind the counter where I could get more flippers as well.

I was munching my fifth cake when the doorbell clanged. Surely it was too early for customers! I had on nothing but soggy trousers. I peeked around the counter, saw a wide-brimmed hat atop a barrel with arms and legs.

The visitor had stopped to catch his breath just inside the shop door. He stood there panting like Matthew G. Perry on a hot day. One hand was empty; the other gripped a sheet of paper. A bill collector! Uncle Slye wouldn't like that.

The man took off his hat and fanned his face. I smelled hair oil. His nose peeked out between his fat cheeks like a squirrel considering coming out of its hole, and his calculating eyes inventoried the room. Then Uncle Slye came through his doorway.

"Phineas Ward," he said, frowning. The man put his hat back on.

I thought, *He needs one hand free to defend himself when he tries to give Uncle Slye that bill.*

Uncle Slye had scarcely grunted his greeting before he commenced grumbling about "that nephew of mine, irresponsible as a cuckoo. Turn my back, he's gone."

That's when I should've risen, only my mouth was full of stolen molasses cake.

"My business is for your ears and mine." Phineas Ward's voice was high-pitched and mean. He shook his paper.

Uncle Slye hurried across the room, glanced at the paper, muttered something, sat down on a flour barrel, and folded his arms.

Ward sat on the barrel next to him, leaned

forward, and began to speak, in a lowered voice now. Still I could make out snatches: "... a *reliable* tip there's a stowaway.... A whole family's run off.... The posted reward's as much for the baby as for the man, fifty dollars apiece. And with the Fugitive Slave Law ..."

Uncle Slye's face remained closed, and his visitor got louder. "My agreement with the owner is, this reward he's posting comes to me, plus half the damages the smuggler has to pay *him*. I'll give you the posted reward if you supply what I need, which is just the loan of enough money to hire somebody to make the trip to South Carolina with me and look after that baby, taking it back to South Carolina."

I grinned so hard I lost some cake. Uncle Slye lend money? When it snowed in August! Which in Newburyport, Massachusetts, meant never.

In any case, this Phineas Ward's offer was a scam. I thought I knew what the Fugitive Slave Law said, and if I was right, catching his stowaway meant big money. I remembered Mam and Father talking in low tones about the Fugitive Slave Law President Fillmore signed a couple of years ago. Among other punishments, such as jail, anybody helping a runaway slave had to pay a thousand dollars to the robbed owner. If I was right, Ward was offering Uncle Slye fifty dollars to help Ward himself get half that *thousand*.

Uncle Slye had to know that as well as I did, and sure enough, he shook his head. But his protest wasn't the one I expected. "No, no. Who'd hand over a fifty-dollar reward for a brat who can't work for years? The man will surely wiggle out of paying. I'll have thrown my money away. Get a tip on the *parents*, and I'll talk to you."

Phineas Ward rattled his paper as if he wanted its words to fly off and smack Uncle Slye on the face. "He knows if he gets the baby, the mother returns. Why waste time and money looking for her, when we already know where the whelp is? Of course, if your brother's so dear to you that you'll pass up—"

Uncle Slye snorted. "How dear have *I* ever been to *them*? Did my parents remember who was their eldest son when they wrote that will splitting everything exactly three ways? Did my brother Thaddeus say, 'You're crammed into two little windowless rooms, Slye. I've got a house in Rockport with a view of the sea! You take Father's house'? Did my brother Raymond say, 'I've got a mansion on High Street, Slye. You take Father's house'?"

I wasn't too surprised by this tirade. I'd heard Father say how furious Uncle Slye was when Grandfather's house was sold and the money split equally among the three brothers. And I'd heard Uncle Slye sneer that people like my family who live on High *Street* think that makes them High *Society*. But my parents don't give themselves airs. For one thing, we never know when a sea storm will cost Father his cargo. We'd have to leave our High Street house if that happened a couple of times.

I try not to think about what would happen if a storm took his whole ship.

"No, you listen to me, Phineas Ward." Uncle Slye leaned forward, his narrow chin stuck out like a spar. "The scofflaw could be my mother, and I'd . . ."

I couldn't hear *what* he'd do, but I didn't need to. Fifty dollars would buy four hundred barrels of flour like the one Uncle Slye was sitting on. Uncle Slye would see *anybody* jailed for four hundred barrels of flour. But I was still surprised that he didn't hold out for more. Some of what Ward said that I hadn't been able to hear must have sweetened the deal some way.

Actually, he'd said more than enough. I guess my brain just didn't want to accept the significance of what my own uncle was saying. That had to come gradually. "Property's property," Uncle Slye wound up. "Nobody's safe if people think they're free to take your property!"

I'd heard better men say the same. Our minister says respect for the law is every God-fearing man's duty. He says slavery's wrong, but so's robbery, and two wrongs don't make a right. He says *thou shalt not steal.* I knew, though, that my parents did not like the law. As for me, I'd have liked to ask Uncle Slye, Who's safe if people can be property?

"No!" Uncle Slye was interrupting Ward again. "Don't do anything right away. Nothing closer than two ports from Newburyport. I mustn't ever be connected with it."

Phineas Ward sneered something, and the paper went back under his cloak. He and Uncle Slye rose and moved toward the front door. "I won't make a cent this morning!" Uncle Slye griped. "That boy has no more loyalty than an alley cat! Where's he got to?" He hadn't welcomed me, hadn't let me touch so much as a penny of a customer's money, but now he was complaining that I wasn't there. Now he wanted me to man the store. He set his CLOSED sign in the front window, and I heard him lock the front door as he and Ward left.

My heart rose that I hadn't been caught eavesdropping. Then it plunged. What was I to do with Allie? I could go to the Chases' and ask to stay with Tom till Mam got home. Tom's mother would welcome me. But she'd never let me bring Allie through her door.

I couldn't stand around thinking about it; no telling how soon Uncle Slye'd be back. I raced up those loft stairs for the second time. Thank goodness, Allie'd licked herself respectable. She chattered as I untied her, as if I were the one to be forgiven. I pulled on a shirt but didn't stop to change to dry trousers, just threw my things into my bag. Knew I should fold the quilt and put it on the counter, but feared to waste a second. Patted my shoulder for Allie to jump up and hustled back downstairs.

Hoped Mam would never find out I didn't empty my chamber pot.

Chapter 3

Nowhere to Go

I rattled the front door, but the bolt wouldn't move without its key—the key that was in Uncle Slye's pocket. How were Allie and I to get out? For a second, I actually thought of throwing Uncle Slye's stool through the front window. "This wouldn't be happening to us if we'd sailed with Father," I moaned to Allie. "And I'm plenty old enough!" I gave the door a kick. "Commander Farragut put down a *mutiny* at twelve!

"He's short, too," I added, not so loudly.

Allie looked impressed. I didn't tell her it was just a one-man mutiny.

I needed to spend less time mouthing off and more time thinking. Such as reflecting that maybe Uncle Slye's back door wasn't locked.

Of course it was—but glory, hallelujah, the key was on a nail right beside the door.

Getting out of that store cleared my mind. "I'm going to find you a good new home," I told Allie. I don't think she understood me, but I didn't have time to tell her the idea that was coming to me. I had to get us away from there fast!

My plan was to take Allie from tavern to tavern till I found another sailor who'd love her the way the first one had. I shoved the question "What if I don't find one?" down to the pit of my stomach where it hurt less than up in my chest. (And willfully ignored the fact that it was going to hurt a lot more if I actually found someone to take her.)

The General Wolfe was the nearest tavern, just a bit farther down State Street. For the first two blocks, I ran hard enough to catch a fly ball. Then I stopped dead.

When Allie throws up, she *throws*. Nothing gets on herself. Everything gets on whatever's two feet in front of her. This time, luckily, it was a bush that dripped.

Allie looked at me wide-eyed. She's always surprised and impressed after the need to puke seizes her. I didn't take time to scold her for being a greedy gut. I paused only long enough to be sure she was through. I dreaded having Uncle Slye catch us on the street.

I was running, but I'd rather have crawled. The thought of giving up Allie made me nearly as sick as Allie'd just been. Still, I knew better than to slow down, even after Allie clapped one scared hand over my right eye. At the General Wolfe's corner, I paused to check both streets for Uncle Slye, then ran up the tavern steps.

I slipped into the noisy, crowded room, making the two of us as small as I could. I didn't know how Mr. Tilton felt about monkeys in his tavern, or boys either. The smoke immediately got Allie to sneezing. I edged back to the wall and let my eyes search for somebody who looked like a sailor who'd be kind to animals. I was encouraged by one man's big-collared middy blouse and the black-varnished hat lying on the table beside his left ear. In that outfit, he had to be a sailor. Unfortunately, his head resting on his folded arms and the empty tankard beside his right ear told me that shaking him wasn't apt to be any use just now.

Allie'd latched on to my own right ear. So many strangers made her nervous. I prayed she wouldn't scream when I gave her away.

I prayed I wouldn't cry. Or at least that nobody would see me.

"She docked this morning," I heard Mr. Tilton's bass voice say. "Hold full of bananas, I'm told." His back was turned our way, but he was quite close, talking to a fellow with long front teeth and longer sideburns, and a stout, red-faced man in a homespun vest.

"Aye, and I heard there was a two-legged spider amongst the stalks," Sideburns answered.

"'Twouldn't be the first time she's carried undeclared cargo, from what I've heard," said Red Face.

"Oh, that's all talk," purred Mr. Tilton, "just talk."

Red Face shrugged. "Well, go down dockside.

Maybe you'll see a black spider hauled out of the *Beauty* with the fruit, maybe you won't. I'm not saying I know."

Startled, I moved a few steps nearer. "Excuse me, sir," I gasped, "did you say the *Beauty?* The *Newburyport Beauty?*"

Noticing Allie and me for the first time, Red Face broke into a grin. "The *Newburyport Beauty,* none other. Would one of you be having a sweetheart aboard her?"

The others laughed, but Allie and I were already halfway out the door.

As we neared the river, the crying gulls, the sparkling blue water, the mingled smells of new lumber and drying codfish brought back the last morning Mam and I had stood on Cushing Wharf, watching the *Black Skimmer* melt away. Now as then, Allie clung to me, both arms tight around my neck. Clearly she sensed my anxiety.

Among the moored vessels, I spied one at Bartlett's Wharf with a long-haired, blue-gowned figurehead. My heart hit my ribs like a cat in a sack. Alongshoremen were unloading crates from this schooner onto Bartlett's Wharf, and I knew the broad-backed, black-booted figure supervising. I ran.

"Ray!" Uncle Thad beamed, his eyes almost shut. He hugged me, Allie on my shoulder and all.

Uncle Thad smells like the same pipe tobacco as Father. The corners of his eyes are even wrinklier than Father's, from more years of staring into the sun. His mustache is thicker and graying; the ends of his sideburns are gray.

"Uncle Thad!" I cried. "They said at the Wolfe you'd docked! Uncle Thad, Father's at sea, and Mam's in Boston. Do you need a good hand? A hard worker? I'm your man!"

Uncle Thad's eyes are blue as a kingfisher. Under bushy lowered eyebrows, they sized me up. And he didn't say a word. I faltered. I'd been sure he'd say "splendid!" He's always spoiled me. Mam says it's because his son who died was my age to the year.

My gut tightened. "I can polish brass! I sandpaper our door knocker every Saturday. I can swab decks to beat anybody; I scrub our kitchen's deck clean enough to suit *Mam*. And I'm limber as hog guts, I swear. I've climbed the *Skimmer*'s rigging all the way to the crow's nest. I've climbed the famous Newbury Elm, and Father says it's near eighty-five feet tall!"

I didn't mention that the *Skimmer* had been moored at the time. I didn't mention the scar on my right arm from falling out of that landmark elm.

Uncle Thad still hadn't spoken.

"This is Allie," I said quietly.

Uncle Thad nodded to Allie. He wasn't smiling anymore.

"Uncle Thad," I pleaded, sickeningly unsure now what he would say, "Uncle Slye doesn't like Allie. Can we sign on with you?"

Uncle Thad wasn't smiling, and I wasn't breathing. His answer, I could see in his eyes, was *no*. What were Allie and I to do?

May 1852

Ogun's mother doesn't speak much Yoruba; his father, none. His grandmother Nana Cora gave him his name: Ogun, Yoruba god of the forge, maker of sword and plow. "You will free your people from the buckra," Nana Cora told the wide-eyed baby in her lap. "And then provide for them."

Ogun's mother calls him her little *awun*, turtle, because he's so sober; her *kékeré òwiwí*, little owl.

The man who tells Ogun to get a move on several times a day calls him Youboy. Long before Ogun began to go to the field every morning, his mother taught him to look at the ground when he is called Youboy and to quickly do whatever he is told.

Nana Cora called him Ogun, always.

Ogun walks home from the field with the other hands. His mother is waiting on their cabin porch. She steps inside ahead of him, stops, and turns to face him as he shuts the door. Mingled with the familiar odors of stale wood fire and staler sweat, Ogun smells pipe tobacco. No one has smoked a pipe in the cabin since Nana Cora was sold off the plantation. His mother has stopped right in front of him; his eyes dart beyond her, searching. Instead of a smoker, they discover the empty cradle. His mother lays a cold, slender fore-finger across his lips. Her own remain closed as she stares unblinking into his eyes, and he realizes that he is never to ask the question that is on his tongue.

When she sees that he knows this, Ogun's mother murmurs, "Sleep in your clothes tonight. Your father has sent for us."

Chapter 4

Into the Briar Patch

llie leaned out toward Uncle Thad, hanging
on to me with one forepaw, trying to investigate
one of his big pockets with the other. Still not
speaking, Uncle Thad reached into the pocket,
pulled out a banana, and gave it to her.

I swallowed. He reached in again and pulled out
a banana for me. I took it, but I couldn't eat so
much as a bite till I heard his decision. "Father's at
sea, and he gave me this monkey," I chattered, "but

now Aunt Lou's packing two babies, and Mam's got to help her, and she left us at Uncle Slye's, and Allie poured molasses all over the floor, and we need a place to go." I told Allie's and my whole story (except for the flippers).

And except for Uncle Slye's hog-fat visitor. Worry about losing Allie had shoved Phineas Ward way back in my mind.

When Uncle Thad finally opened his mouth, he was frowning. Allie's life depended on his answer. My right hand slid up and gripped her right foot so hard she nipped my thumb.

"Can you milk a goat?" Uncle Thad asked.

I stared.

"Can you?"

"Yes, sir," I answered, a little sullenly. Usually I enjoy Uncle Thad's joking, but I surefire wasn't in the mood for it now.

"Good. Then you can milk our goat and do anything else Cook wants. Welcome aboard." He shook my hand as though we were standing at the head of the *Beauty*'s gangplank.

"Allie too?"

"Allie too."

Saved. Allie was saved! Nothing had ever meant more to me.

"Her rations will come out of your pay."

Pay? He was going to pay me like a regular crew member!

But milk a goat? "Do you really have a goat?"

"Cook likes fresh milk, and a cow takes up too much room. Now, we'll unload a few more crates here, then we're catching the first wind for Salisbury. I'll take your uncle Slye a free stalk of bananas before we sail. He'll forgive us, I think. And I'll tell him to tell your mother where you are when she comes for you."

Ordering me to get Allie out of his store, Uncle Slye'd been like Buh Wolf throwing Buh Rabbit into that briar patch Cora told me about. I followed Uncle Thad aboard in a state of bliss. In my excitement, I forgot how short Buh Rabbit's happy spell in that briar patch turns out to be.

Building the *Newburyport Beauty* had taken Uncle Thad's life savings. I was popular the day she was launched: Everybody got out of school to watch. She's a flat-bottomed vessel, three masts, plus the spar that sticks out over her figurehead like a narwhal tusk. "In front of Mam," I told Allie, "Father calls that spar a bowsprit. Otherwise he calls it the widow-maker, because of all the sailors who fall off bowsprits." Allie's eyes got big. "Cooking," I reassured her, "doesn't involve the bowsprit."

She didn't look convinced.

Sometimes she's smarter than I am.

The *Beauty* sails from coastal port to coastal port, delivering practically anything. She's no clipper ship, but feeling her roll and toss under my feet was a thrill, and later when the white sails were all loosed at the same instant, my chest filled to bursting. The biggest Yule tree the city of Newburyport ever lit didn't come up to that moment for dazzle.

The *Beauty*'s long-haired, pink-cheeked figurehead stares dead ahead with the very look our minister's wife gets when listening to him sermonize. She was carved to see the *Beauty*'s crew safe to shore; she'd never lead anybody into half so many adventures as the fierce bird that flies ahead of Father's ship, I warned Allie. "But she beats Ingle's Groceries all hollow!"

Allie seemed to agree.

"Come along. I'll introduce you to your mistress," Uncle Thad said.

Tied to the mainmast was a brown goat with eyes the color of the amber necklace Father brought Mam from Saint Petersburg, Russia. "We call her by the name her mother called her," Uncle Thad said. "Ma-a-a-andy."

Then he presented Allie and me to Cook: "Most important man aboard!"

Of course that's really himself, but Cook knew the introduction was at least half true. "A bad cook means a bad ship," Father says. "Discontented crew. Slacking. Fighting." Judging from Cook's goose-belly, I figured he must be pretty good.

Cook is tall and, except for that gut, spare. With his long, bony face, narrow chest, and big belly, he reminded me of the long-handled gourd squash Mam grows, except he's black, not yellow. He didn't seem overjoyed to be getting a helper. I'd expected a big smile; I'd thought that his wife, Cora, would have told him all about nursing me when I had flu. I'd even had a moment's mind picture of the two of us laughing together over Cora's story, "How

Sis Nanny Goat Got a Short Tail." But of course if Cora did talk about me, she wouldn't have mentioned Allie. Cora'd never laid eyes on Allie. Probably Allie put Cook off, I decided.

Uncle Thad went aft to his cabin, and Cook showed me around, introducing me to the rest of the crew as we went. Mate, Uncle Thad's second in command, wasn't the one Uncle Thad had brought to Mam's Thanksgiving dinner when the *Beauty* was in port last November. Uncle Thad had told me that our Thanksgiving guest, Hiram Upham, "fell out of the apple tree in his parents' backyard a few months ago and broke his ankle. Caught it in a fork, and snap!"

Hiram Upham was lucky that Uncle Thad had known him all his life and hired just a temporary substitute until Hiram could walk again. "Little bone like this fibula will heal in a few months," Rockport's doctor swore.

Of course, if Hiram were really lucky, his parents wouldn't have asked him to spend his rare day ashore cutting a dead branch out of their tree. "Lucky," I've told Allie, "depends on when you take score." She didn't look as if she disagreed.

The *Beauty*'s temporary mate was a pigtailed, freckled Irishman from Rockport, with a back as broad as a shield that looked as if anything you threw at him would just bounce off it. I wondered how he felt about his temporary status. He was in too much of a hurry to join Uncle Thad to waste time on more than a grunt to me and Allie. But he had time after only a few strides to pause and say something I didn't hear to a man untwisting old rope for seam caulking, something that ended with the louder remark, "There's nothing poisons a vessel like the captain having a pet aboard!"

I knew I was intended to hear that, and I knew Mate didn't mean Allie. That minute I resolved to stop saying Uncle Thad and start calling him sir and Captain.

The other four crewmen were Newburyporters: first the Plumer twins, Tim and Jim, so thin you could tie them in knots, but both strong as the rigging they climbed quick as spiders on their own thread.

"Tim's the one with the beard," Jim told me. The beard was the color of the tar he and his brother were applying to the sheets. "I had one every bit as handsome, but Mate makes me shave so he can tell us apart."

Right away I bet myself that Jim would stop shaving the day Hiram Upham came back aboard. Hiram had known the Plumer twins since they were boys and wouldn't confuse one with the other in the dark.

I noticed that Jim didn't quit tarring rigging while he talked, and that though the brothers eyed Allie, they didn't slow down and invite conversation about her. It was the same when I met the other two crewmen. I told myself I'd better keep that in mind too.

Phil Wood, even taller than the tall clock his grandfather made my great-grandfather, looked up from the hemp rope he was untwisting, shifted his quid just enough to let him speak, and said, "Knew yer gram. Give me a marble one Sunday. Green."

Grandmother, Mam's told me, used to give a marble to her Sunday school boys when they could recite the assigned Bible verses. I wondered what she'd have thought of the half-naked mermaid tattooed on this Bible student's arm.

The fourth crewman, nicknamed Hawk for his

eyebrows being jointed like osprey wings, was stitching a sail on the fo'c'sle deck. "Hawk Currier," he said. "Welcome aboard." He stood and shook my hand. And he didn't bend his back at all to do it. I liked him.

Turned out that Hawk was part of the big family who own Currier's shipyard in Newburyport; they built the *Beauty*.

We were standing beside a sliding hatchway, the one the crew climbed through to take the ladder down into the fo'c'sle, where they ate and slept. "You bunk with the crew," Cook said. Then he led us back to the main deck and the door to the galley.

The space at the bow under the *Beauty*'s fo'c'sle deck is divided evenly lengthwise by a pine-board partition. The fo'c'sle is on one side of this bulkhead, and the galley's on the other. Cook's expression soured as we approached his galley door. I began to wonder if it was only the monkey on my shoulder he minded. "Nobody," he paused to say before opening the door, "*nobody* allowed in the pantry that opens off'n the rear of my galley but *me*. You just freeze onto that, Ray Ingle, if you want to live long and die happy!"

So, I thought, *Cook's another Uncle Slye, afraid somebody'll snitch a cracker.*

"You gon' eat with me in the galley," Cook grumped. "You'll carry the captain's meals to his cabin, and Mate's. And you'll fetch their dishes back and wash 'em."

Cook slept in a hammock suspended from hooks overhead in the galley. I was surprised to learn this, for the pots hanging on the galley wall made a constant clatter as the *Beauty* dipped and rose. I didn't think *I* could have slept through it! "Stinks in the fo'c'sle," Cook stated. "A cook need to smell what he cook. Sleep in that hole one week, you couldn't smell a pig."

The crew got served their stews and such in big wooden tubs called kids. Cook showed us a little table-height sliding door in that bulkhead between the fo'c'sle and the galley. Through it I would pass these filled kids. "And you'll get 'em back *empty*," Cook assured me. This bulkhead's boards were warped; cooking smells wafted through. The crew,

I soon confirmed, was always more than ready to eat when that little door opened.

In spite of his grouchiness, Cook couldn't hide his delight that he wouldn't have to cramp his thighs squatting to milk that short-legged little goat anymore. "Quit when you got about a cupful," he instructed me, handing me a small pail.

Short-legged myself, I got on fine with Mandy. And I wasn't afraid Allie would wander off into mischief while I milked. Just as when she'd watched me milk Tom Chase's goats, she was fascinated by the miracle my hands were working.

Like Cook's delight, that was nice while it lasted.

Chapter 5

Black Spiders

As I stood up to carry Cook his milk, Hawk Currier came to ring the first dogwatch, four strokes on the great brass bell attached to the *Beauty*'s mainmast. Mandy was clearly used to this bell that shared her post. I was to learn that she didn't seem to mind anything, so long as she had hay to munch. Allie put her forepaws over her ears.

A landlubber might have thought the ship was on fire, but from spending all the time I could aboard Father's *Skimmer* whenever she was in port, I understood how a vessel's bell divides each day into six watches. Beginning at half past midnight with one ring, the bell gets struck every half hour from one to eight times, one stroke being added for each half hour passed. At eight strokes, the count starts over. The four A.M. shout down the hatch, "Eight bells, d'ye hear the news?" was the work-day's beginning for most of the *Beauty*'s crew. "You and me," Cook had told me right off, "rise and shine at seven bells!"

Decks get scrubbed during morning watch, which ends, none too soon, with breakfast at eight. Break-fast to noon is the forenoon watch, followed by dinner and the afternoon watch. After that, four to eight P.M. is split into halves called the first and second dogwatch. I was offered three different explanations by three different shipmates for this nickname, none the same as what Father'd told me.

Eight P.M. to midnight is the first night watch. I slept every minute of it, after my first day as Cook's helper. Midnight to four A.M. is the mid watch, and that was another story.

Allie'd been obliged to make herself comfortable

on my stomach again as at Uncle Slye's, this time because my bunk was so narrow. "You'll be glad it's narrow if we hit rough weather," Hawk told me. "When the *Beauty* gets a-rollin', we'd be pitched on the floor if we couldn't brace knees and backs against our bunk sides." I gloried in that "we."

I'd feared Allie's snoring would annoy my mates. No need. The sound that bunch sent up through the hatch made the *Beauty*'s foghorn sound like a kitten. But after very few minutes, I wasn't hearing them or Allie either, as the long ocean swell rocked me to sleep.

I woke in a cold sweat. Swarms of hairy black spiders covered my chest, crawled over my bare arms, my face.

Lord be praised that I didn't scream—of course it was only Allie. Allie, and Red Face's "maybe you'll see a black spider hauled out of the *Beauty* with the fruit."

I'd slept right through the mid-watch call, but I didn't sleep again, for now came thoughts ten times worse than my nightmare. What had I been thinking of all afternoon? Mam always accuses me of "going off half-cocked." Would she, would anybody in the family, ever forgive me for my slow fuse this day? Would *I*? How could I have failed to tell Uncle Thad about Red Face and his talk of "undeclared cargo," Phineas Ward and his "reliable tip"?

In the tavern, my great anxiety had been finding a place for Allie. The gossip I'd overheard hadn't seized my mind the way the *Beauty*'s presence had gripped it. Now my guts knotted into a baseball. What if there was truth behind that gossip? What if there really was a runaway slave aboard Uncle Thad's vessel? And what if Uncle Thad knew it? If the law showed up with Phineas Ward and found the black stowaway that Red Face had hinted at and that Phineas Ward was sure of, Uncle Thad would be ruined. He would get out of jail in six months, but to what? He might not be disgraced in the eyes of people like me and Mam and Father, but he'd be penniless.

I ought to have warned him before ever I stepped aboard. Joy that I wasn't to lose Allie after all, rapture at being allowed to sail at last had put everything else out of my mind.

That we were sailing to Salisbury was public knowledge, and now we were so near Salisbury, there was nowhere that Uncle Thad could make up some excuse to dock first, give a stowaway a chance to steal off, not even swimming. I remembered how Phineas Ward had sneered when Uncle Slye told him "nothing closer than two ports from Newburyport." I hadn't heard Ward's answer, but I didn't necessarily trust him to stick to it anyway, whatever it was. If only I'd spoken, even as late as after sundown, Uncle Thad could have assigned the night watch to a man he could trust—surely there was at least one such man aboard? He could have assigned the night watch to that man, and the four of us could've lowered a boat, let the stowaway row for his life. I didn't try to think how we'd have accounted for the missing boat in the morning. It was too late for that scheme anyhow. Too late. My fault. If Phineas Ward's search party met the *Beauty* as she docked at Salisbury, there'd be no way to keep them off her. They would find anyone aboard.

Maybe not. Maybe Uncle Thad could think of some way to pass off a stowaway as a crew member. I could suggest that to him! I wanted to jump up and run to the captain's cabin. But there was no way I could waken Uncle Thad and not Mate. If there really was a stowaway and Mate didn't know it, then the big mouth that Mam's always suggesting I keep shut might be as dangerous to Uncle Thad as a search party. I didn't know what Mate thought of the Underground Railroad; I didn't even know what he thought of Uncle Thad. But Allie, I'd noticed, was afraid of him. I couldn't suppress the feeling that it would be a mistake to risk everything on the chance that Mate was a good fellow. I lay miserably clutching Allie for comfort, waiting for the seven bells that would release us. Even then, it would be hours more before Cook would send me to the captain's cabin with breakfast. But at least I would be moving.

Apparently Cook took only about four minutes to throw on his clothes and trice up his hammock. He stuck the little milk pail at me as I entered the galley, saying, again, "Quit at about a cupful." Allie and I hurried to where Mandy was penned under cover between decks at night. I milked by lantern light. "There'll be no more grooming each other first thing every morning," I told Allie.

That baseball I was toting around inside me had turned to lead. I felt a sharp hope when Mate left the cabin at eight bells to boss the crew, but this turned out to be no help after all, because the minute I handed over the milk, Cook gave me another task.

When Cook finally ordered me to carry Uncle Thad and Mate's breakfast to the quarterdeck, my guts began to quiver like sunlight on waves. This was not an improvement over the baseball.

Mate beat me to the cabin door and held it open for me. I set my tray down on the table in the middle of the cabin, saluted Uncle Thad, swallowed hard, and left. Back to the galley and my nonstop silent prayers. I didn't have much appetite for breakfast.

Allie lit in.

The minute we'd eaten, I had to scrub Cook's bowls, pots, cups, and ladles, plus the crew's kids, and cock them all carefully outside the galley door to sundry. Then—hallelujah!—just as Cook sent me for the cabin's dirty dishes, Mate emerged. When we met, he didn't say a word, just scowled and strode past me for the fo'c'sle deck. There he stood bellowing orders at the Plumer twins, who were hanging on with their eyelids while they tarred rigging with both hands.

I stepped into the cabin. Never had I so dreaded something I'd been praying for.

gun's tenth birthday. The usually silent marsh had vibrated that evening with the hollow, booming roars of a bull alligator. "He calling for to mate," Ogun's father said. As he spoke, the gator roared again, and they saw him stretched out on his own little island, his jaws gaping so wide it looked to Ogun as if he could swallow them both and their boat besides. Ogun had seen an alligator capture a grandfather turtle once, crushing shell, bone, gristle, and all with one snap. "The Yemassee who live here before the white man come call the alligator 'Fish-Like-a-Mountain,'" Nana Cora had told Ogun. Only in their language it was *Nanneb* something; Ogun couldn't remember. He worried about forgetting. He feared that he might forget his grandmother's face the way he'd forgotten his grandfather's.

A cool April, still the marsh stank of decay. Water

moccasins dangled from live oak branches overhanging the black water; now and then one dropped, sliding quietly in. To Ogun, some of the branches themselves looked like snakes. He lowered his line into the water, and the bit of fatback tied to its far end sank out of sight. Ogun imagined himself sinking like that. This water was so snaky, he had never learned to swim.

At the other end of the boat, Ogun's father rested his oars and bent to reach for his own line. As he straightened up, the bull stopped roaring.

The way he'd been bellowing, no wonder he was worn out. But even as Ogun thought this, the alligator splashed into the water, sending out great waves that rocked the boat, though it was a fair distance from the gator's island. A night-colored bird that Ogun hadn't noticed before flew up and away with deliberate wingbeats and harsh protests. But the gator swam silently, powerfully, directly toward the boat.

Ogun had lived by this marsh all his life and never been menaced by an alligator. But Ogun's father dropped his line onto his seat, rose, and seized one oar again. "He think this boat be alligator," he said quietly.

The gator reached them astonishingly fast. His silver green eyes looked as big as Ogun's fist. They were glaring, furious, their normally slitted pupils wide as the moon. He rammed the little boat so hard it shipped water. Standing, oar in hand, Ogun's father swayed with the boat. Ogun held on to his seat, praying for both of them.

The alligator swung around and came at the boat again, his long mouth open wider than a fireplace, his teeth too many to count or even guess how many—dozens of them, sharp, wet, and shining. Ogun's father rammed his oar so far down the alligator's gullet that Ogun feared to see him lose a hand, but the jaws clamped shut on wood. "Tie his muzzle!" Ogun's father commanded.

For a second, Ogun thought only of his fishing line, but remembered the boat's thick rope before his father had to shout at him. Every nerve shrinking, every second expecting to lose an arm, he wrapped this rope round and round the gator's muzzle and tied it shut.

"Tell everybody come help," Ogun's father commanded, then recalled that his son couldn't swim.

Ogun had to stand and hold the oar while his father first swam and then ran.

Everybody on the Street ate alligator stew for Sunday dinner, and Ogun and his father were heroes. Ogun received the alligator's right hind foot—his, he was promised, forever.

All wistful memory now. Even if they had a boat and oars, Ogun and his mother aren't going to kill a gator with Ogun's makeshift kitchen knife. Thrown out broken by the Big House servants, this knife had been rescued by Ogun, who then sharpened what remained of its blade with a rock. It is sharp, but not very long.

As for gator eggs, May is too early. Ogun and his mother have come upon two nests, last year's, empty, their rotting smell the smell of the marsh itself times ten. The last piece of corn bread got divided first thing yesterday. No lunch. "We not missing meals," Ogun's mother told him. "We just putting some off for a while." And come afternoon, Ogun had killed a squirrel, stunning it with a rock from the slingshot he'd stuck in his waistband just before they'd stolen out of their cabin and wringing its neck before it recovered enough to bite him. (Only a white man goes hungry in the woods, Ogun's father told him early and often.)

Ogun is proud of this slingshot, which he made himself, a long strip of young vine with a leather patch in the middle. As he whirls it around his head and lets the stone go, he pretends that he is David slaying his ten thousands, or himself, slaying the man who calls him Youboy.

By the time he'd skinned his squirrel, Ogun had been hungry enough to try to eat it raw. This hadn't been necessary, thanks to the tinderbox in his mother's big skirt pocket. Even with no salt, they'd enjoyed that squirrel, and Ogun felt as proud as the night he'd tied the alligator muzzle shut. But today, drizzly rain is keeping every bird and small creature hiding. Ogun scrabbles grubs out of the dirt, pokes snails out of their shells, swallows them whole. His mother chews, but throws up the first grub Ogun gives her before she really finishes swallowing it. After that Ogun wraps each of hers in a leaf so she can pretend it's something else.

If he'd been able to keep his lucky alligator foot, the sun would be shining, Ogun broods. "Take only what you can carry running," his mother had cautioned him. In the end, things she considered more useful than that precious foot took up all Ogun's space. He's glad he at least insisted on the slingshot, though it digs into his midriff when he runs. Will there be alligators in Canada?

They have to keep walking, rain or no. Someone is to meet them, his mother swears. They must be where she promised, when she promised, rain or sun. Ogun hopes whoever she promised feels that way too.

Chapter 6

Banjo Music

ncle Thad had shoved the breakfast dishes aside and was studying a huge chart spread out on the table. The thought stabbed me that it was good he was seated, in case what I had to tell him gave him a heart attack.

When I have a report that's hard to make, I take a deep breath, fix my gaze on the listener's collar, and talk fast. I left out my stealing and eavesdropping and just told in general terms what

I'd heard at Ingle's Groceries and at the tavern. Finished, I wished I were sitting down myself.

Studying Uncle Thad's face, I could tell nothing about his thoughts. He got out his tobacco, then just seemed to study it awhile. Finally he looked at me. "Don't be worrying, Ray. Every time this vessel's about to leave harbor, any harbor, I go over her from stem to stern. I can assure you, there isn't one person aboard who isn't entitled to be here. I can account to God or man for every soul she carries. Don't worry about Phineas Ward, or tavern gossips either."

"Right, sir," I said. All of a sudden my bowels relaxed; Allie just had to hang on while I raced straight from the cabin to the head. Not that the *Beauty* has one. We backed up to the headrails. *Splosh.*

"Father says everybody did this in the old days," I told Allie. "We just say 'the head' for short— which everybody also did in the old days, Father says." The ocean makes a privy that never has to be cleaned.

Now I felt empty of worry as well as of breakfast. Uncle Thad's assurance that the *Beauty* was safe at least took some of the pain out of telling him that his own brother was willing to ruin him. Now I could relax and enjoy my first Sunday at sea. Nobody pinching my cheek. No sermon (if you don't count the seagull that was going our way, took a brief rest in our rigging, and squawked non-stop). No rule against smiling or singing or telling tall tales not in the Bible. When Cook sent me to the quarterdeck with midmorning coffee, Uncle Thad was smoking the long clay pipe Father had brought him from Holland. Not even a back-yard in Newburyport permits lighting a pipe on Sunday.

"The Sabbath was made for man," Uncle Thad remarked, his voice solemn but not his eyes, "not man for the Sabbath."

His manner told me that he was quoting, so I tried to answer "yes, sir," as if I recognized the quotation. Then I hurried back to the galley. I wasn't forgetting Mate's "nothing poisons a vessel like the captain having a pet aboard!" I was con-scious that my last visit to the cabin had lasted longer than would've been necessary just to collect a tray of emptied dishes. I needed, as Mam likes to counsel, to "avoid the appearance of evil."

Cook immediately sent me to milk "about a cup-ful," again.

"The goat I milked at home got milked just twice a day," I ventured. "And I was told to be sure to milk her out every time, or she'd dry up."

"Captain like he coffee milk *fresh*," Cook snapped.

I hurried away to Mandy. "Why didn't I stop to think?" I worried to Allie. "If I rile Cook, then you and I could be put ashore at Salisbury and slapped on the first train for Newburyport and good old Uncle Slye!"

Allie just went on grooming my hair. I hoped nothing would fall into Mandy's milk.

As I returned to the galley with my just-a-cupful, I heard an old-squaw, that duck that sounds like a sobbing baby. To my surprised pleasure, Cook instantly sent me up to the fo'c'sle deck to see if I could spot the fowl.

Nothing flying, roosting, or swimming. Allie and I stood gazing down at the foaming trough the *Beauty* plowed, so high the bowsprit shone slippery wet. I shivered. "You see that sort of giant spider web made of rope," I said to Allie, "hanging between our figurehead and the bowsprit?"

Now, Allie's dried-up, wrinkly pink face and big white beard may make her look like a wise old man, but she can be as dumb as a rock. Why in the name of the thirty-one states did I point? In a swallow, Allie was *down* from my shoulder, *up* on the top headrail, *off* leaping for the bowsprit. There she held on with feet, hands, and tail, riding up and down as the *Beauty*'s bow rose and smacked, rose and smacked.

"Allie!" I yelled. "Get back here!"

She lifted her chin at me and grinned her ears almost off.

I gripped the headrail so hard my knuckles turned white. I knew Allie. Any more yelling from me and she'd show off worse, and good-bye, Allie. Scooting to the galley to grab a bribe was out of the question; she'd surely be in the drink before I got halfway across the fo'c'sle deck. The night before, Cook had sent me to dump the supper garbage, and I'd seen the first shark show up just seconds after the splash. I'd thought back then to Father telling Mam and me how sharks detect motion in the water miles away, how the more a poor drowning sailor struggles, the more sharks rush to savage him.

I jammed a hand into my pocket, made a tight ball of my handkerchief, then held my stuffed fist up so Allie could see I had something in it. "I've got something for you!" I called. "See what I've got for you?"

With a leap no human could manage, she just made it back. When she saw I had only my handkerchief, she scolded like six angry squirrels, but I wasn't in the mood to apologize. "You want a shark to eat you? Huh? You want to drown? You listen to me! Uncle Thad lost a man off that bowsprit just the second time this schooner sailed! That man and the Plumer twins were lashing the jib down. A wave reared up just as the bow dipped, and that man was gone. *Swallowed*. I don't want to see you playing on that bowsprit."

The next time Uncle Thad had walked down the gangplank onto a Newburyport dock, he'd carried under his arm plans he'd drawn for something he wanted Currier's shipyard to see to immediately.

"Uncle Thad figured out how that web we're looking at could be put on the *Beauty*, and she didn't sail out of Newburyport again till it was in place.

"That web would catch a man who got knocked off the bowsprit, but *you* would fall through. There'd be shark jaws crunched around your head before you could even scream. You stay off that bowsprit."

Clam Hopkins called the web a fishnet, jeered that Uncle Thad had decided to go into whaling and didn't know how. "Ole Thad Ingle's gon' be a big-time whaler," he cackled. From that day on, if the *Beauty* put in to Newburyport, Clam demanded, "How many whales didjer uncle catch this trip, Shorty?" and laughed like the idiot he can be.

Uncle Thad went to school with that drowned man's father when they were boys. He doesn't care about being laughed at.

Allie seemed to think the handkerchief should be hers, that I'd promised it to her. I handed it over, and she threw it over the side that instant. She wanted an apology, I guess, but she didn't get one.

"Gone, see?" I pointed. "That's just how long you'd last if *you* fell in!"

Years ago, when I was too little to have good sense, I never let my hand dangle over the edge of my bed for fear a shark would leap up and grab it. Good thing Father doesn't know this—I might never get to sea. But I wouldn't mind making Allie that cautious!

When Allie and I returned to the galley without so much as a keepsake feather, Cook was in the pantry, with the door shut as always—playing his banjo! It wasn't for me to even think about what Cook should've been doing. I got to work peeling potatoes. "We need to shore up our standing with Cook," I told Allie. When Cook came out, he found me with a knife and a nice heap of newly white potatoes and Allie busily scraping at a still perfectly brown one with a spoon.

Cook rewarded us by sending me off to scout the crew for something to read. "Sunday be the day for that on this here schooner. Next time you come aboard, Ray, bring you some books." I liked the sound of that "next time." Maybe I was forgiven for shooting my mouth off about when to milk a goat.

I wished I had the Shakespeare play Mam had been reading to me and Allie every night before Aunt Lou's letter arrived. *Richard III.* We'd just got past where the Duke of Clarence gets drowned in a wine barrel. A big fight was coming up.

None of the crew had *any* Shakespeare, and even if Uncle Thad did, I was afraid to encourage Mate's resentment by borrowing a book from him. Hawk Currier had a two-day-old *Newburyport Herald.* I'd never taken much interest in the paper ashore. Now I borrowed Hawk's copy and took it up on the fo'c'sle deck, where the light was brighter than any place ashore ever gets, and Allie and I pored over every page.

One notice caught me. A reward was posted for a slave family: man, woman, boy, baby girl. For the return of any one of them, fifty dollars; two hundred dollars for all four. Surely this was the very notice Phineas Ward had shaken at Uncle Slye. I smiled to know that it didn't concern us, that I didn't need to show it to Uncle Thad. He'd already reassured me that the *Beauty* wasn't involved.

Phineas Ward and all the rest of those bounty-hunting hounds who might read this notice were no threat to us.

Allie, who always minds when I seem not to be thinking about her, pinched my thigh. I gave her tail a tug and moved on to reading the report of William Lloyd Garrison's latest speech about how every slave should be freed instantly.

Mr. Garrison used to be the editor of the *Newburyport Herald*, till he printed something rude about one of our merchants. Since he got out of jail, he's lived in Boston. Clam Hopkins says, "That lunatic Garrison not only favors turning Africans loose on us, he wants to let women vote! He didn't stay in jail long enough."

Tom Chase and I've talked about Mr. Garrison a few times. We both agree with him that slavery is a poison, but Tom says there's no need to give women the vote. "They'll all just vote the way their husbands do," he says. "You double the voting line but get the same answer."

I told him right plain he doesn't know Mam. But about slavery, yes, she does feel just like Father and me.

Mate happened to tramp by and look over my shoulder while I was reading. Just the name in the headline set him off. Mate seemed to agree with Clam. He flipped his pigtail front to back and talked and talked (which was like Clam too). His face got so flushed you could scarcely tell he was freckled. "Why doesn't Garrison make a speech about the slaves in Newburyport's cotton mills?" He didn't stop even for breath, let alone an answer. "How far did he live from those mills—an eighth of a mile? A quarter? But never did he notice the men like my pap who worked in 'em. The boys like me . . .

"Younger'n you I worked in the mill, tied to my machine so's no quitting, not for any reason. Before dawn to after sundown. One freezing day, I fell asleep on my feet, and the foreman threw cold water in my face, soaked my shirtfront. 'The faster you work, the faster you'll warm up again,' he said. Next day I shipped with the first captain would take me."

Mate had my sympathy now. I opened my mouth, but his voice never paused.

"I sailed a boy, but I came home a man. A good

thing, because Pap had died, they said of pneumonia. He died of hunger, I tell you. Because I'd run away, the mill fired him. Blacklisted him so no other mill would hire him. If my mother hadn't had a brother in Rockport to take her in, she'd have starved too. Garrison didn't print a word in his paper about *that*." Mate spat over the side and walked on, his feet thumping as if the oak planks were so many mill owners.

I was left with my mouth hanging open, staring after him. "We're lucky he didn't spit on Hawk's paper!" I told Allie once I began to breathe and swallow again.

Later, walking past Mate and Hawk on the fo'c'sle deck, I heard Mate growl to Hawk, "Well, any black stowaway I ever found on a tub I was aboard would right quick find himself swimming! I'm not going to jail for somebody else's halo. Captain wants to go to heaven, let him arrange it on his own time." I'd guessed right about Mate. I had to keep walking, so I didn't catch what Hawk answered him.

At twilight, Cook got his banjo, sat down on the windlass, and commenced strumming, singing along in a lazy bass. The Plumer twins had the watch, Jim on the wheel, Tim on lookout, but the rest of us gathered around, leaning on the railing, lying on the deck, or sitting on a rope coil. Hawk and Phil both turned out to be tenors. I didn't think Mate would sing with us, but seems he's proud of his baritone. I was sorry for Uncle Thad, who couldn't join us because of having to be the captain.

Some songs nobody knew except Cook, but we all sang "Oh, Susannah," "Barbara Allen," and "Haul on the Bowline." My voice has started to crack once in a while, but it didn't betray me this time. I climbed down the ladder into the fo'c'sle with the crew that night as happy as I'd ever been in my life.

Reporting to the galley before dawn Monday, I found Cook brewing coffee for the men who'd be going on watch at eight bells. As usual, he sent me to milk "about a cupful." (I kept my mouth shut.) At first light, he sent me to help the crew on deck. Anything, I thought, to get me and Allie out of his galley.

"Leave them shoes below, Ray," he advised.

The head pump had been rigged, and seawater

was rushing everywhere as the crew washed decks. I was handed a mop. Allie didn't like the water. She sat on the deck rail and scolded, which got everybody laughing. We scrubbed, scraped, sanded. I thought of how I hate it when Mam makes me scrub our hearth bricks, but this, with my shipmates joking around me, was fun. (Funniest was after the decks all shone spotless as our sails and I brought Mandy up to tie her to the mainmast for the day. Before I could even fetch her hay, *rattle rattle rattle*—her little manure pellets were hitting our gleaming deck.)

For nearly four hours we had worked like firemen putting out a blaze. Nobody made conversation at breakfast!

Immediately after we ate, I was back milking Mandy again, my head resting against her side. Allie'd taken her observation post as before, atop the nearest rope coil.

Maybe she got jealous of Mandy. Maybe she got bored. Whatever the reason, off she went, and I didn't notice. Until, that is, I heard the laughter of several men from the direction of the fo'c'sle deck and Allie shrieking as if she had her tail in a vise.

Chapter 7

A Thief's Fate Aboard

Allie's shrieks would have woken a drunkard. What in the name of Jehoshaphat were those apes doing to her? I jumped up so fast I almost knocked the milk pail over.

What I saw was like being plastered between the eyes with a raw egg. Allie, sitting on the windlass, was holding a frying pan just like Cook holding a banjo, tapping her foot like Cook, and screeching.

Hawk and the Plumer brothers were watching this performance, laughing so hard they were lucky they didn't fall down and roll overboard. And charging up the fo'c'sle deck's port ladder was Cook.

I shoved the pail out of Mandy's reach with my foot and lit out for the fo'c'sle deck's starboard ladder. I didn't even glance toward Cook—just snatched up Allie, frying pan and all, and fled.

"Don't be jealous, Cookie," Hawk called, wiping away tears. "True, she plays as good as you, and she's just as good lookin', but she can't sing worth nuthin'."

Cook's scowl would have routed the Barbary pirates.

How had Allie sneaked that pan out of the galley? Cook must have been in the pantry, was my guess. The answer wasn't important. What mattered was that when real trouble cropped up in the galley, neither Allie nor I had any reserve credit left with Cook. We were already in bad.

Cook continued sending me for milk several times a day. There wasn't much in our cooking, and nobody took it in his coffee but Uncle Thad, who didn't use so much as a pint a day. "I think I know where Cook gets his paunch," I told Allie.

I was climbing the rigging any chance I got, so my own belly was getting hard. Likewise the soles of my feet. I was leaving my shoes off, not just because of morning deck-wettings, but because for climbing, you need to be able to grip the ratline between your big toe and its neighbor. I was determined to be so quick in the rigging by the time Father came home that he and Mam would have to admit I was seaworthy.

With all this climbing, I was like Matthew G. Perry, world's hungriest dog, ready to eat anything anytime. Making buns Tuesday morning, Cook scowled at my expression as I opened the *Beauty*'s thirty-pound raisin box. "Start whistling, boy," he snapped. I had to whistle the whole time I was measuring out raisins for him. "So everybody know you ain't sneaking any. Sea custom." He whistled himself, till the final precious raisin was stirred in and the box firmly closed. Allie watched with big eyes, but I never saw a chance to slip her even one.

The buns came out of the oven perfect, brown as mushrooms and just as light. Cook set them to cool, and we went above, Cook to smoke his pipe, I to polish brass, Allie to lean against the bulwarks and play with her tail. We were beating our way up the coast; the wind in our sails was music that made work a pleasure. I started with the windlass and proceeded aft. I polished the great bell until, when Allie finally joined me, she put me in stitches, making faces at her ghostly reflection.

My laughter was choked off by a roar from the galley. Moments later, Cook appeared on the main deck. I hadn't seen anybody so mad since the day Tom Chase and I hid Clam Hopkins's pants while he was swimming. "Eight! I make eight buns! Now I only got just *five*. Where they go, them three? You think bun *walk*?"

Rations are a big issue under sail. Sailors must get equal shares. The *Beauty* makes frequent stops, restocks her larder often. Nobody eats maggots or goes hungry as if she were crossing South America's fearsome Cape Horn, say, or worse, becalmed. Fairness at mess is vital, though. Cook was as upset as if the crew'd performed Shakespeare's drowning of the Duke of Clarence, casting his banjo as Clarence.

The Plumer brothers were picking oakum, converting old hemp ropes into caulking for loose seams, near enough to Cook for him to see them laughing. They didn't laugh at dinner when they were two of the three shorted a bun.

I was the third.

It took me a while to realize what this should've told me.

Just before dark Tuesday, Allie and I took Uncle Thad his day's final coffee. Mate was at the wheel, not that I cared. I now had nothing to say to Uncle Thad that I couldn't say in Mate's hearing.

The thought that Uncle Thad might have something private to say to me didn't even cross my mind.

Uncle Thad's bunk and Mate's run fore-and-aft, Uncle Thad's on the port wall, Mate's on the starboard. Uncle Thad's desk is in the forward end. Seated at the desk, Uncle Thad seemed to be taking inventory of his medicine kit. He didn't greet Allie and me so heartily as usual, and his blue eyes looked as lackluster as the Merrimack River on an overcast day.

Thoughts of needing any of that medical stuff were depressing him, I figured.

"I have to check this kit once in a while," he remarked. "Doesn't do to wait till a man falls off a mast to find out your laudanum's half dried up."

"No, sir."

"I was on a clipper once whose second mate had chained himself to laudanum through the years. Nobody knew it till the cook laid a hand open with a cleaver and there wasn't a drop of painkiller aboard. Captain put in to the nearest harbor; a tornado wouldn't have blown him there too fast to suit him. Not just to get care for our cook, but to get that second mate off the ship." Uncle Thad paused and looked at me. "Because a thief aboard a vessel never makes it home."

He paused again, his eyes holding mine. "There's a splash in the night. Nobody sees anything. Nobody hears anything. It's sea law. Even on his own vessel," he said heavily, "a captain cannot protect a thief."

With a shock I realized why he supposed I needed

this story. It was a warning. Cook had been up there carrying on about his buns, his three whole missing buns.

I opened my mouth to state that nobody need fear any petty theft from me. Uncle Slye's flippers popped into my mind, and I paused. Maybe Uncle Thad caught my guilty look, for his mouth tightened.

But it was a good thing I had, for once, closed mine. What I'd been about to swear could've shifted Uncle Thad's suspicion to Allie. Of course there were five others on board who might've snitched a bun, but Allie and I were the newest. We were the convenient suspects.

Allie being only a monkey to Uncle Thad and Cook, the two of them might not even wait for a second theft. The Plumer twins had been pretty mad about getting shorted on buns. I imagined them cheering as poor little Allie plunged to a terrible fate.

Uncle Thad spoke a few fill words to end the interview. His voice sounded sad and stern. I couldn't follow what he was saying for my shame and indignation. I stumbled back to the galley and slammed down my tray. Luckily, Cook was in the pantry.

"I wish we'd never set foot on the *Beauty*!" I raged to Allie. "Why didn't we just hide out at home? I know where Father's front door key is."

Mam's so afraid she'll lose her key while Father's in midocean and have to hire somebody to force our lock that she hides Father's key under the mossiest rock in our garden. "There's not a Newburyporter I'd suspect of housebreaking, Raymond," I've heard her say to Father, "but there's no sense paying somebody to practice."

"With all Mam's laid by in the cellar," I told Allie, "you and I could live in our house for a year and nobody'd be the wiser!" But sure enough, I'd gone off half-cocked again, leapt aboard this bigbeamed schooner, and, though I didn't tell Allie so, now our lives were in danger.

I wished Uncle Thad and I'd had our talk before supper; I'd have taken care not to drink a drop. What if I needed to go to the head before dawn? I could be gone with a splash, never even knowing who'd murdered me.

I didn't dare venture up on deck in the dark. I wondered if I dared sleep.

May 1852

"Yenta me, yenta me, yenta me," the frogs drone.

Ogun has jammed a stick into the bank, but the vines in his hands won't stay braided. Every time he makes a good start at turning them into a rope, he has to blink. Then when his eyes reopen, the rope has unraveled. The pieces lie in his lap, useless as ever.

Ogun had watched his father braid vines, back before his father walked off right in time to miss Ogun's birthday. Vines had never given Ogun's father any trouble. Ogun's are like chickens that won't be shooed. Every time you think you have them going into the pen, they dart another way. When the vines somehow escape his lap, Ogun just goes ahead and puts his father's hat on the stick. His father won't hold it against Ogun if an alligator knocks the hat into the marsh. He'll be proud of Ogun for remembering this trick.

The stick is shorter than Ogun. Placed on it, the top of the hat comes just to his chin. An alligator's unlikely to attack a man, but he'll go for a boy quick enough.

And quick enough one comes, charging, roaring, more terrible than a tornado. It's what Ogun desired, yet he shrinks in fear, and now he remembers that he has no rope, no way to lasso the alligator that is hell-bent for his decoy. Wildly Ogun looks around for the vine he'd been trying to braid and wonders how he could have missed seeing the nest he is standing on. But when he cuts an egg open, the tiny alligator inside bites his thumb and the pain is so sharp that he drops the egg and awakens.

He opens his eyes with a sinking feeling. Everything that had been true when he closed them is still true. He and his mother are still, for all he knows, lost, though his mother says not. They are still hungry, tired, sore. What will happen to them if they're caught? What will happen to their bodies if they starve to death in these woods? Would his father ever know that they'd tried to reach him? Ogun imagines his dead body being chewed on by feral hogs, but his mind recoils, refuses to imagine such a fate for his mother.

His mother. He is supposed to be getting them something to eat, something for supper. He'd sat down to get a stone out of his left shoe, that's all. Has he slept more than a minute or two? Has his mother noticed?

It's not quite dark yet, and she's sitting nearby, just watching him. "Yenta me," the frogs drone. "Yenta me, yenta me."

At a stream Ogun breaks off a shadbush shoot and chews the end to make as sharp a point as he can manage. He hates the way the frog he gigs looks like a tiny naked man—a tiny tied-down naked bleeding man. But he is hungry. He makes another spear, and he and his mother each roast one leg. Intending praise, his mother as she eats says, "You my real little man." Ogun winces at that "little." Ogun the Provider sees himself a man, period. But they stop chewing, or even breathing, when they hear the high, excited yelp of a hunting dog that has scented what it seeks. One dog, and then another, maybe three dogs.

Someone is hunting raccoons. Or someone is hunting runaways. "Come!" Ogun commands, and his mother drops her frog's leg and leaps up. "Throw it in the water! Run!"

Frantically Ogun scrapes dirt over their tiny fire. Every yelp sounds nearer. No use to climb. A 'coon dog knows all about treed prey. They begin to run.

Chapter 8

The Man on the Dock

uesday night I lay awake. Who did swipe Cook's sacred buns? Mate seemed the likeliest villain. He was the newcomer; he hadn't been aboard a whole great lot longer than me and Allie. "People who feel sorry for themselves feel entitled to get what they consider some of their own back," Mam says. Mate felt sorry for himself because of the mills.

Mate also felt more powerful than anybody else

aboard, except, of course, Uncle Thad. "I'll bet Mate thinks the rules don't apply to *him*," I whispered to Allie. Allie put one paw over my lips. Whispering displeases her. I blew her paw off (well, actually I nipped it a little) and squinched my eyes in hopes of sleep and no nightmares.

There wasn't much joking as we sanded decks Wednesday morning. Nobody laughed or even looked me in the eye when Allie snatched one of the smoothing stone's ropes and tried to help pull. I focused determinedly on my work. If anybody wanted to glower at me, he could do it for his own entertainment; I wasn't acknowledging.

Cook never had been warm to Allie and me, so there wasn't much change in the galley's atmosphere. As for when I took Uncle Thad and Mate their breakfast, I was too ashamed of what I thought Uncle Thad was thinking to look him in the face, and neither he nor Mate spoke to me.

It was the same when I took them their dinner.

Cook continued demanding unreasonably frequent milkings. In between, he had me slicing, chopping, dicing, and mincing enough onions to feed a fleet. He seemed amused at the way this tortured my eyes, more amused, even, than when he'd first noticed my scarred thumb.

My left thumb is scarred from whittling a model of the *Black Skimmer*. Mam wanted to confiscate my pocket knife with my blood undried. Luckily, Father came to my rescue, asking, "Why take away his knife now he's learned how not to handle it?"

Cook's comment when he noticed my ridged thumb had been, "It be the dull knife that slip and cut you, boy. Not a blade in my kitchen won't cut an *eyelash*." Too bad he never set me to slicing eyelashes. I chopped onions Wednesday till my eyes felt poached.

Around ten Thursday morning, we docked at Salisbury. Cook had assigned me so much chopping that I obviously wasn't going to be able to leave the galley for even a quick look over the rails. I had a feeling this was his misplaced revenge for those stolen buns. When I thought about that, I had to be extra careful with the knife.

Cook himself was going ashore to grub up. He gave me a scowling lecture as he stepped out of the galley. "You remember what I done tole you about my pantry, Ray Ingle! If you so much as open the door, I will know. I have ways." Muttering, he took himself off.

I waited just long enough for Cook to step onto the gangplank to jab my knife into an onion and march straight to the pantry.

As I reached for the door, I felt Allie lean forward on my shoulder. My arm dropped. I could just see Allie leaping away from me into Cook's precious sanctuary and in ten seconds making the kind of mess she'd made at Uncle Slye's. Some things you can't put back the way they were before an ornery monkey got to them for even an instant.

What did I care about Cook's stupid pantry anyway? Ignoring Allie's protests, I turned my back on the galley altogether and sneaked up to the rail for at least a *look* at Salisbury.

My punishment for this look was an immediate shock. Standing mostly behind a stack of bales on the dock was a barrel-shaped man in a wide-brimmed hat. Apparently he was watching who came ashore from the *Beauty* and who boarded. The *Beauty* shuddered as she struck the quay pilings, and so did I.

But after my hair lay back down, I smiled. I almost hoped it *was* Phineas Ward, as I'd thought for a second it was, almost wished he *would* fetch the law and come aboard, get himself hot and dirty searching for someone who wasn't there. Go down in the hold and find a banana spider. Not the kind yabber-jabber Red Face meant, but the real hairy, eight-legged kind that can kill you with one bite.

At this thought I smiled again, spat over the rail, and beat it back to the galley.

Allie seated herself on a potato sack, as far from my onion fumes as she could get and still keep an eye on me. Cook came aboard with meat, laughed at both of us, and next set me to cutting up the meat. "Sea pies for supper!"

Briefly I considered asking him if in crossing the dock he'd noticed a barrel-shaped lurker who stank of hair oil. But what difference, I asked myself, would it make if he had? "Least said, soonest mended," Mam's always reminding me after I've blurted out something again.

Allie seemed even more pleased than I was, watching Cook set eight sea pies in the oven. She knew I would share my pie with her, but she wasn't the one who was going to be washing eight pie pans.

The pies came out perfect. Cook set them to

cool, then sent me to report to Mate. I wondered if he was afraid I'd swallow one of his precious pies whole. The heat of the oven in that small galley had me sweating. Being treated like a thief made me hotter yet.

Earning my keep in the galley, I'd missed seeing the magic moment when the *Beauty* spread her wings, though I'd heard Mate shouting his commands, heard the crew chanting as they hoisted anchor, heard the sails snap as they filled. Now Salisbury and the glimpsed figure I'd mistaken for trouble were well behind us. Good that I hadn't made a fool of myself, running my mouth.

On the fo'c'sle, Mate directed me to the capstan, which is a large, spool-shaped device for hauling up sails and anchors with the cable that's wrapped around it. Capstans work like the pulleys on farm wells, except they go round and round instead of up and down. The cable wrapped around the capstan is always rusty, and scraping cable is what Mate set me to. Allie settled herself to snooze in the capstan's shadow.

The smell of saltwater cried, *The world is wide!* Those pies murmured, *And it's good right here.* At sea at last. The sky a perfect blue. The *Beauty*, as she plowed the water, favoring me with a cooling spray. I should've been sing-and-dance happy, but on my knees on the fo'c'sle, I brooded about the injustice of my fix. In disgrace for a crime I didn't commit, afraid to defend myself to the person whose good opinion I needed right now more than anyone else's in the world.

Of course what I should've been thinking about wasn't the injustice of my fix but the danger.

I recognized Mate's tramp coming up behind me without turning my head. (Mate's every step announces that where he's set his foot is now *his* territory.) But I turned my head right fast at his words.

"Leave off that dallying. Gaps in the bowsprit's man-catcher."

I felt the hair on my neck rise up like Matthew G. Perry's when a bigger dog makes a noise in its throat. Any gaps Mate had noticed in Uncle Thad's web, someone was going to have to go out on the bowsprit and mend, and I was being called on to lend a hand in some way—I couldn't think how. This would be a one-man job, surely, and I didn't even want to watch. My lungs would barely be working the whole time anybody was on that bowsprit. Seeing somebody fall into that merciless ocean, never to come up, was not what I'd so eagerly signed on for.

"Don't set there gawping like a guinea hen, boy. Up with you."

I glanced around as I rose. Nobody there but me and Mate. Even Allie'd disappeared. Gone into hiding the minute she saw Mate heading for me, it looked like. She'd shown signs of being afraid of him before. Now suddenly I was afraid of him myself.

Nobody at all was on the fo'c'sle. Hawk, Phil Wood, the Plumer twins, all were far aft and high in the rigging. Uncle Thad apparently was in his cabin, Cook in his galley. A chill crept up my spine and seeped into my shoulders. Slowly but unstoppably, it flooded down both my arms, past my elbows, to my fingertips.

I was the one being sent out on the *Beauty*'s widow-maker. Alone.

Chapter 9

Hanging On to Life

stared down at the bowsprit. Was this how they planned to drown me? In broad daylight?

Even Hawk, who'd seemed so friendly, did he know what Mate was up to?

Did they all?

Or was this entirely Mate taking advantage of a spell when everybody was somewhere else? Mate who'd sent them somewhere else himself!

Mate who'd copped those stupid buns and

figured that if he drowned me, he could come right out and say I'd done it.

Did anybody ever murder for a stupider, stupider reason?

Did anyone ever *die* for a stupider reason?

Mate was already striding forward. I tried not to stumble, following. Glancing over the side, I saw the ocean as a giant, foaming-mouthed shark, just waiting for me.

When we reached the bow, Mate produced a handful of short rope pieces. I took them silently, tucked them half inside my waistband, dangling half free, so I could easily pull them out one at a time. Uncle Thad's contraption is like the net that circus acrobats use in training. Basically, the drawing he'd taken to Currier's shipyard had shown perpendicular lines attached across the foremast stays. Standing beside Mate at the bow, I could see that he was right. Constantly strained, wet, grinding each other, three of the connections in this web now had given way, enough to leave a gap a man could fall through. Let alone a boy. A *short* boy.

My job was to cobble up those gaps, make the web effective till it could be dried out and properly spliced. This cobbling would have been one whale of a lot safer in port, where we were soon due! There wasn't an icicle's chance in a bonfire that Mate wasn't familiar with how hard it is to knot wet rope. His impatience made no sense, unless safety was exactly what he didn't want. I studied his face. "I need a safety line," I ventured, but Mate spoke over me.

"Move yer feet. Quit stallin'."

I reflected that a safety line wouldn't do me any good if the man at the other end untied it, and fear swept through me again. And that made me furious. Without another word, I hoisted myself up onto the headrail and dropped down onto the deadly bowsprit.

The moment my feet hit wood, the jib swung straight at me. My toes gripped white-hard as I ducked to a crouch, and when I could breathe again, I silently blessed my bare feet. They were bare, and I wasn't drowning (yet) because of Cook's advice the first morning he sent me to help the crew. Maybe Cook was regretting that good advice this minute, knowing what Mate was up to. I could see him in that galley of his, playing his banjo to celebrate my fate. Wondered what he'd do to Allie if I did drown. I could guess.

I'd never cottoned to the *Beauty*'s blue-eyed fig-urehead, and now as I gazed down at her thick tresses, I downright disliked her, knowing how she would unblinkingly watch me plunge to my death. Breathing hard, I lowered myself onto my stom-ach, laid my cheek against the spar, held on with my legs, and reached down to grab at the net. I took the first high wave smack in the mouth. As I jerked back spluttering, choking, I was saved from falling by the death grip of my knees and thighs. After that I took many a blinding wave in the face, but I kept my mouth shut.

The bowsprit angles up a little, a small gesture toward protecting a man working on it from the bow's rhythmic dipping into the sea. When it came to working on the net below the bowsprit, though, this angle was quite the opposite of help-ful, making the reach more of a stretch. I found myself edging more and more off the spar until I was hanging on to life with my legs only.

Mate, as he'd handed me his rope lengths, had suggested that I might find my work easier if I lay in the net itself. That made sense, and I was about to try it, but something came to me that Dr.

Spofford had said to me once, reproachfully. It was right after he'd set the arm I broke falling out of the Newbury Elm. "Whenever you're about to take a chance, Ray, remember this: God forgives always; man, sometimes; nature, never." If three joints in the net had already rotted, who knew where else the net was about to separate, stressed by a sudden burden? Even the burden of a very short boy.

Maybe that was exactly the thought in Mate's mind. I looked down at the grave awaiting me, and little points of light danced before my eyes. Swallowing hard, I went to work where I was. As I watched my hands reaching toward the first web gap, I couldn't stop imagining the razor-toothed shark that I would never see until it had taken one of those hands off in one bite. And now I kept hearing Father telling Mam and me, "A shark that smells meat will leap higher than the Newbury Elm to get it."

Of course I was soon soaked from crown to heels, and what was worse, so were the lengths of rope I was trying to weave patches with. I wrapped one slippery end of a length around what felt like a still-sturdy web line, knotted it, then stretched its other equally slippery end across the gap to the next sound but dripping web line, and wrapped and knotted again. Now it was Father I silently blessed. How angry with him I was, the morning I proved I could tie every knot he'd shown me! Was I praised and rewarded? "Ships don't stay dry," Father'd said, and set a pail full of water and more rope lengths beside me. "Now tie me all those knots again," he'd commanded, and gone out into the garden to smoke his pipe and, I felt certain, laugh.

How I'd wanted to upend his bucket right over his feet, to kick his shins. How I'd struggled to tie knots with those accursed wet rope pieces. Impossible, I'd thought first, and second. But I'd done it. I'd learned. And now, if a wave didn't get me or the jib, if Mate didn't throw something to knock me off my spar, if a white shark didn't leap out of the water and tear me in two where I lay the way Father saw happen to one of his crew in the Bay of Fundy, I was going to do it again.

Over and over, I tied a piece of rope across a gap, then crossed it with a second piece in the other direction, over and over. I have no idea how long the job took. Long enough that when the time came to rise, my hands were bleeding, and I had to wonder if my legs could relax their grip on the bowsprit, if they would prove too shaky to support me as I made my way back along the slippery, bobbing spar to the headrail. At least while I was lying down, no sail's vicious sideswipe could hit me with all the strength of a runaway horse, sending me into the cold gray water without even the hope of a big-mouthed, big-bellied whale.

As I lay there nerving myself to try to rise, the *Beauty* took her biggest plunge yet, and I was totally under water. I wasn't conscious of embracing the bowsprit; my arms did this without my bidding. With both arms and both legs, I clung to life, blind. Not seeing, not breathing, not even praying.

Up out of the water we rose—and down again. The ocean had one will, the plunging schooner another, and a third time would have been too much for me, too much for my arms, for my legs, my nose, my lungs. Then one or the other, vessel or ocean, eased. Eased just enough, just long enough, for me to breathe, to know that to continue to cling to that life-sustaining spar was suicide, to prize first my arms, then my legs, apart. And rise.

On tingly legs that felt as full of bubbles as a glass of ginger beer, I made it to the headrail, hopped down at last onto the fo'c'sle deck. Hawk was there as well as Mate, and he reached out a broad hand to steady me. From his perch high in the rigging, he must have seen me go over the rail and had hit the deck and hurried forward, then waited. Was he as suspicious of Mate as I was?

Water collected around my bare feet as I stood shivering like a beggar in January. "You look a little green around the gills, sailor," Mate said. That "sailor" was a compliment! I did my best to grin.

It was good to have flat boards under my heels, but I wasn't triumphant yet. I had to reassure myself that Cook or somebody else hadn't decided not to wait for me to drown, hadn't hurled Allie off the *Beauty's* stern the moment I set foot on her bowsprit.

As my eyes began to sweep the decks, a howl from Cook himself got the attention of every man aboard. I jerked around to see Allie come shooting out of the galley and make a flying leap for the foremast ratlines. Not a foot behind her was Cook, the galley's biggest cleaver in his upraised hand.

May 1852

Some black men didn't have to go to Canada like Ogun's father to be free. Some black families, whole black families, were free already, didn't have to go to Upnorth at all. Ogun's mother doesn't say how she came to know of such a family, and Ogun knows not to ask twice. He's satisfied to have slept last night on a rug made of cotton strips instead of on damp Spanish moss, to have gone whole minutes without slapping at a hundred mosquitoes, to have been urged "take another bowlful!" instead of "save some for tomorrow, now," to have sat in front of a rocking chair after supper and listened to a story told right out loud instead of straining to understand his mother's hand signals, both of them afraid to make a sound. And ahh, to breathe the lovely smell of their hostess's pipe, that smell that was his grandmother's, washing Ogun with successive waves of bliss and sorrow.

"So that's how Sis Nanny Goat's soft heart got her a short tail," Ogun's hostess had concluded. She hadn't told the story exactly the way Ogun's grandmother always told it. Anyone Ogun had ever heard tell Buh Rabbit stories told them a little differently from everybody else. Nana Cora had told the best stories on the Street.

Ogun's mother claims that the white man who bought Nana Cora and took her away was sent by his grandfather, claims his grandparents are living together, free now, but Ogun doesn't believe this. Comfort is his mother's job; Ogun is old enough to have caught on to that.

Ogun had been proud that children from up and down the Street would come to sit on Nana Cora's floor with Ogun and listen to why Buh Frog has a hump on his back (Buh Wolf bounced a knothole off it, that's why); how Buh Rabbit and Buh Partridge fooled each other playing hide-and-seek. But there was one thing about her storytelling that Ogun minded: She never would explain a story. "You think on it," she'd say. "It'll come to you." But it didn't always.

Why alligators have crinkly backs, for instance. Nana Cora claimed that way back, when alligators had backs as smooth and shiny as butter, Sis Alligator asked Buh Rabbit what Trouble was. Buh Rabbit promised that if she met him by the marsh same time tomorrow, he'd show her. Ogun understood the next part Nana Cora told, where Sis Alligator puts on her bonnet, and the little alligators say, "Ma, Ma, kin we go see Trouble?" and she tells them to go ask their pa. And their pa says, "Go ask your ma." And the little alligators run back crying, "Ma! Ma! Pa say we kin go see Trouble!"

The closer Sis Alligator and her children get to the marsh where Buh Rabbit's told her to meet him, the less comfortable they are. "Ma, Ma, Trouble warm."

"Yes, chile, Trouble warm."

Then, "Ma, Ma, Trouble *hot.*"

"Yes, chile, Trouble hot."

Until finally, "Ma! Ma! Trouble BURN!" and Sis Alligator cries, "Yes, chile, Trouble BURN!" and they all plunge into the black marsh water to escape the fire Buh Rabbit has lit, and their lovely butter-smooth backs sizzle and pop and crackle, and that's how come alligators have crinkly backs.

But why did Buh Rabbit do them that way? And why did Sis Alligator have to ask him what trouble was in the first place? Ogun has known trouble all his life.

Trouble right now is not knowing just where they are to get on the *rél ùweé abẹ́ ilẹ̀*, as his mother swears they will do. Everybody on the plantation but Nana Cora spoke Guinea. Once she was taken away, Ogun stopped learning Yoruba words, but he knows those four: They mean "under ground rail way"—the way that his mother promises will take them far enough from here that they can never be brought back. But there's been no railway, aboveground or below. They've just been walking, walking—north, if the stars can be trusted. Ogun has the unvoiced fear that maybe the stars are somehow ruled by the white man like everything else. Maybe the white man can mix up the stars to fool people like him and his mother, lead them here or there, anywhere but north to freedom and his father. Ogun's feet hurt; his shoes were already snug when he was given them, and that was last November. Everybody on the plantation gets measured for new shoes every November and every May, but only the foot's length is taken, never its width. Trouble is sore feet.

Today's way, through a virgin longleaf pine forest that smells like rest, is a rutted clay loggers' road. The sound of approaching horses stops Ogun's musing about what trouble is. In the deep shade of these ancient pines there is no underbrush to conceal them, but perhaps better than brush, the pines have never been pruned, and their branches begin at the ground. "Climb," Ogun urges. His mother is already reaching up, grabbing hold. They fight their way as high as the branches seem likely to support them. Then they cling and wait, grateful that the tall pines are too thick to shake with their fear.

Chapter 10

Sad Duty

I forgot my soaked clothes. Lunging after Allie, Cook fell flat on that big belly of his. The cleaver he'd been brandishing skittered away—but not far enough! Allie, climbing with one paw and both feet, had reached the boom by the time Cook was back on his feet. Her other paw gripped a pie.

Cook no sooner caught his breath than he recommenced howling. One hand retrieved that meat cleaver, the other was a fist. Dancing at the foot of the mast, Cook shook both.

How fast would a cleaver that could split an eyelash lop off a tiny monkey's head? Allie scampered to the end of the boom, wrapped her tail around it, and swung off into space. Dangling by her tail, she was free to grip her pie with all four palms, and to feed it into her face as fast as pouring milk out of a pail. She did pause now and then to grin.

A monkey's grin doesn't mean *ha ha*. It means *reach for my pie and I'll take your hand off*, but Cook didn't know that. "Go on," he screamed. "You go right on! Uh-huh, you laugh. Wait till you come down. We find out how hard you laugh under water!"

High on their masts, all the men stopped working to watch Cook dance and Allie eat pie. Even Mate permitted himself to exchange a grin with Hawk; even Uncle Thad in his cabin heard Cook's shrieks and came up on the quarterdeck to investigate. He stood erect, keeping a captain's dignity, but I know Uncle Thad. He was laughing inside.

At least now he'd realize that I wasn't the thief, I thought resentfully, then felt myself flush. How ready had *I* been to think that Uncle Thad was risking the roof over his family's heads, just because a wheezing tub of lard with stinking hair told my other uncle so, a tub of lard and a couple of tavern dawdlers? How ready had *I* been to think that Mate was not merely a thief but a would-be *murderer*, just because he doesn't sweet-talk? Just because he wants to make sure I don't slide by on being the captain's nephew?

"How long you think you float with your gut full of pie?" Cook was screaming. "Sink like a stone!"

Catching an unwilling monkey is dangerous, but nobody's going to catch a monkey up a mast anyway. The crew laughed harder every time Cook yelled. "Funny, huh? Funny? How wide you gon' smile when you the one don't get any pie come suppertime?"

I prayed they'd all feel a belly laugh was as good as a belly stuffed.

"We'll see." Cook's threats lost steam as he wearied. "We'll see how everybody laughing now like *monkey pie*!"

"It's your own fault, Cookie," Hawk teased,

wiping away tears. "Ought to know a smart monkey like Ray's can count. She seen you weren't going to give her no pie at supper, so she took care of herself."

Cook rasped a hoarse retort, which I won't risk repeating before I've left home for good. (I value my scalp.)

Well. Uncle Thad could put his fears for the family honor to rest, but what about my fears for my shameless monkey? Was I going to have to stay awake all night every night to protect her? "Please don't drown her, Cook," I begged. "Just leave her to me. If she ever swipes another thing, you can throw us *both* overboard. I promise. I'll see she never steals again."

"I promise *you*, boy. Don't you worry. *I* promise *you* she'll never steal again!"

Cook stamped back to the galley once Allie ate the last mouthful of pie. Allie came down, and Cook missed observing what I judged was the whole pie go over the side less than a minute later. I'd been expecting it. Size for size, she'd gobbled enough to keep a boa constrictor asleep for a week. And when she starts jumping around right after she's stuffed herself, she spouts like a whale every time. Then she passes out.

I was still feeling hollow-kneed and queasy myself, not to mention sopping wet, but I hurried to the galley to try to placate Cook. Allie wouldn't have the strength to get up to any mischief for at least an hour, I calculated.

But appeasing Cook took more than any hour. Never mind my raw hands, my soaked clothes. I scrubbed every shelf in the galley. I scoured even the pan bottoms till they shone like the windlass. I was about to drop before I got Cook's promise to give Allie and me another chance.

He didn't ask how I was going to keep my vow. (I had no idea.) He said only, "All right, Ray. But the next thing missing—the next *raisin*—and that she-devil is *gone!*"

Now what? I couldn't work, sleep, and have an eye on an active monkey twenty-four hours a day.

Cook needed only a few hours of cooling off before he could describe his embarrassment at Allie's hands (and feet) in triumphant terms; how he'd stood in the pantry holding its door open just a crack and thus had seen the thief hop into the galley and snatch. (There Cook stopped, not caring to relive how Allie'd dashed out again, pie in hand, the second he'd moved.) But I didn't need to know all or any of that. What I needed to know was how to stop Allie's thieving.

The answer I sought came slowly, like mist rising on Plum Island. It didn't make me happy.

First, I needed Cook to leave me alone ten, maybe fifteen minutes so I could hunt for Allie. (I suspected that after all she'd been up to, she'd found herself a corner and collapsed.)

Just being left alone wasn't hard. Seemed like Cook had to go in the pantry for something half a dozen times an hour. Sometimes he was gone so long I had to wonder if he was sneaking a nap. Sometimes I could hear him strumming away on his banjo, singing to himself. But other times it was just in and out quick as a hummingbird. I never knew how long any particular trip was going to be.

During one, I managed to dump some of Cook's hottest red pepper on a square of paper and twist the paper's corners together to make a little package. With that in my pocket, one swipe of lard was all I was going to need more. A swipe of lard and the chance to use it.

As long as I was in the galley, Cook's remaining pies were safe. Fear came when he sent me to get "just a cupful" of milk.

I'd never milked so fast, praying all the while that Allie was plain unconscious, exhausted from all that zipping up and down. Not to mention first taking in and then putting out a pie meant for a man.

The minute I delivered the milk, Cook sent me to the cabin with Uncle Thad's knock-you-down-smelling coffee.

Uncle Thad was writing in the *Beauty's* logbook. His eyes danced as he greeted me. I set down the tray so hard the milk sloshed. "Cook said no dawdling, sir!" I lied, and fled. Allie was surely somewhere between me and the galley, and that was dangerous.

As I rounded the mainmast, the realization jerked me that I hadn't been looking *up* for Allie, just around. Maybe she was taking refuge where she could count on Cook's never following. I stopped dead and tilted my head back as far as it would go.

Bright sun and a moderate wind had done for the morning's gauzy fog. The sails were so white, my almost-blinded eyes looked down again at once—and spotted Allie.

She was curled up in the port jolly boat. I ran for the galley—and when I burst through its door, Cook was in the pantry, talking to himself.

One sideswipe of my hand got me all the lard I needed, and I smoothed the place where I'd swiped so Cook wouldn't notice it. With a lardy right hand and Cook's hottest pepper in my pocket, I stole out. If Cook beat me back, I'd say I'd had to go to the head.

I sneaked up on Allie, in case she was wary of me as well as of Cook.

She wasn't. Our minister says animals have no souls. When it comes to Allie, I don't believe that, but it did look as if she had no conscience. Her wicked face was pink and toothy as an innocent old woman's as she favored me with her sweetest smile. Clearly she didn't dream for a moment that I might be mad with her. I patted and stroked her back with my clean left hand. Her tail, I rubbed with my right. She groomed my hair in return, patted my cheek, and went back to sleep. I peppered her now-lardy tail so she wouldn't be inclined to lick the lard off. I felt like Judas. I hoped Allie'd never realize that I was the one who'd betrayed her.

But if she ever complained, I'd point out that she at least got the pleasure of eating a pie, even if the pie didn't stick with her long. I supped on all the sea biscuit I wanted, thanks a ton.

At second dogwatch, Cook as usual left the galley for his pipe. I sneaked down to the hold, borrowed a bunch of bananas, and laid them on the cooling rack that Allie had twice robbed. Then I went and leaned against the mizzenmast.

Having lost her pie, Allie needed only to thoroughly waken to be ready to eat. I didn't have to wait long.

"All right!" Cook's voice cried. Several others whooped.

Not all right, of course. Up the foremast and out on the boom capered Allie, bananas in hand. Way too late, there rushed into my mind Father's description of how Luzon Islanders catch monkeys. "The hunter drills two holes in a coconut," Father said, "hollows it and baits it. He runs a cord through the holes and ties the coconut to a tree. He cuts a slit in this coconut shell big enough for a monkey to get his empty hand in through it, but not big enough to let a fist that's full of bait back out. A monkey slips in a hand, then won't let go of what he grasps. He sits trapped by his greed till the hunter comes back and kills him for supper."

The thought that Allie might be that stupid stopped my heart. She'd be smashed to death before my eyes . . . and it would be my fault.

Overhead, Allie waved her prize. The crew didn't have time to gather for the fun, Cook didn't even have time to threaten before my little monkey wrapped her greasy tail around the boom and pushed off.

oooooo

May 1852

Before sundown, Ogun and his mother huddle in a white, Bible-quoting farmer's barn. Ogun's mother collapses into sleep at once. Ogun lies down with his head under the cow's udder and milks one teat straight into his mouth. His stomach at ease for the first time in days, he resolves to remain awake, on guard.

He is wakened by a scream.

A bat swooping down from the rafters for its own meal has brushed his sleeping mother's face, segued into her nightmare. She scolds herself; she's plenty used to bats.

Ogun has never feared bats. He knows them for weak, foolish creatures. He tries to remember the bat story Nana Cora told him when he was small.

Once man had no rest, he thinks he recalls. The sun shone all day and the moon shone all night, and nobody ever got to lie down in his cabin and sleep. A basket of darkness was given to Bat to deliver to the moon, Nana Cora said. "Put out she light!" Bat was instructed. "Give man some chance to put down he hoe." But Bat got tired of carrying that basket of darkness, it was so heavy, and he laid it down so he could fly around and catch tasty insects awhile.

A monkey saw the basket. Monkeys are curious about everything, and she opened that basket right away. Some darkness rushed out. Bat hurried to close the basket again, but he couldn't catch the darkness that had already escaped. He took the moon what was left, but it wasn't enough to make the world all dark all night every night. Sometimes the moon is as bright as day. And foolish Bat is so ashamed that he never leaves his hiding place when the other animals can see him. He flies around only at night.

Ogun's mother urges him to lie back down and sleep. They should both get all the rest they can. But the moon is high, and Ogun can't get back to sleep.

And a good thing, for in a very little while he hears men's voices, and when he looks out, he sees that there are two of them, and they are approaching the barn, and they have dogs.

Chapter 11

The Pantry

Head down, Allie plunged toward the deck. Even Cook froze.

The bananas hit first.

Allie, as she plunged, had grabbed hold of a stay with one paw. She swung for an excruciating moment, then had the sense after all to drop her booty and grab the ratlines with the other paw. After that, scrambling down the ratlines was nothing for her, and when she judged the distance safe, she leapt for the deck.

She lit running, but not fast enough to save herself.

Every sailor in sight was laughing as hard as the last time Allie'd scampered aloft with loot, but this time they were laughing at Allie, not at Cook. And they laughed harder when Cook beat me to her and whacked her on the rump with her own dropped bananas. She screamed top voice, which everybody but me seemed to find hilarious. For a horrified instant, I thought she was going to whirl and bite Cook. He'd throw her overboard then, for sure.

I said a thankful prayer as Allie chose flight over fight. She made a dash for the jolly boat where I'd found her napping, and Cook was smart enough not to follow. My shipmates wiped away their tears and got back to work before Mate could roar at them. I wanted to comfort Allie, but Cook wasn't satisfied yet. He trumped up some galley task for me, and the day was beginning to cool before I could look for my pet.

She didn't hear me coming. She was wrapping

her tail around a deck rail. Peering over her shoulder, she slowly, gradually pulled away. Her tail slid off, of course. She couldn't seem to believe what was happening. She tried again. And again. I tiptoed away.

Sharing a bunk with a greasy-tailed monkey wouldn't be my first choice, but it beat hearing Allie hit the waves. I wanted that lard to stay on her till she got convinced her tail was ruined forever, bewitched. I was afraid the lard would be all wiped off on me and the bunk by morning, but I was so tired, and Allie was so subdued by her shock, neither of us stirred.

Of course the lard didn't stay on Allie forever. For one thing, anytime Allie thought nobody was looking, she would wrap her tail around something and test it. But that didn't matter. She never swung by her tail again the whole time we were aboard the *Beauty*. She never stole again, either.

Raisin duff was Sunday's treat. Cook and I stirred flour with simmering water until we had a thick mix, then slid the pot off the heat and, whistling, added raisins by the fistful. Raisin duff was served with molasses, and raisin duff kids always came back to the galley scraped clean.

Cook left me to stir the pot while he went (where else?) into the pantry. Allie was still careful about how close she got to Cook but endlessly curious about anything *I* did. Cook being out of sight, up onto my shoulder hopped Allie, to peer into the big pot as I stirred. The duff had stopped steaming, and the next thing I knew, one hairy forefinger reached in for a taste. If I quit whistling long enough to tell Allie what I thought of that, Cook would charge out of the pantry and accuse me of snitching raisins. So I just jerked the shoulder Allie was perched on.

Allie reached in a whole paw. I jerked my shoulder again, harder. Simultaneously the *Beauty* heaved, and Allie fell face forward into the duff.

For once in my life, I didn't blurt something that made matters worse. (All we needed was for Cook to come running!) Instead, I started whistling shriller and faster than ever, and hauled Allie out by her tail.

With my free hand, I swiped her nostrils. Allie

shook her head, wiped her eyes, and sneezed. Then, calmly, she began to lick around her mouth.

She could have made a meal of what was stuck to her hairy body, and if I'd had time to give her a choice, that's just what she'd have chosen. ("Monkeys are like cats," I remembered Father swearing to Mam. "They keep themselves clean.") Instead I knelt with her on the floor, whipped off my shirt, and, ignoring her protests, cleaned her cleaner than she'd been since Mam left for Boston. I'd *just* got the last duff out of her belly button and stood up when the pantry door opened and Cook rejoined us. I balled up my shirt and threw it into the farthest corner.

"What's that filthy rag on my clean floor?"

"Shirt's too hot. Stirring duff's hard work."

"Huh. Today's nothing. Can get so hot in here, spit boil in your mouth." But he didn't order me to put my shirt back on.

Nobody complained about the duff at supper. I didn't find any hairs in mine, anyway. It tasted all right to me. Probably the molasses helped.

Sunday night I had such wild dreams I was glad

to wake up. Unable to get back to sleep, I eased out of my bunk without rousing Allie and climbed to the deck. Neither cloud nor moon was showing up to compete with the stars, and the sky looked like Mam's plum pudding after she's sprinkled sugar on it. Hawk had the watch aft and let me take the wheel awhile, standing behind me, his hands over mine. "You don't need no compass tonight, Ray. Pick you out a star that's in line with all three masts and keep her there."

The sea was calm, the *Beauty* sailing directly before the wind. After a few minutes, Hawk took his hands away and the *Beauty* was mine. She moved as I moved; we were one body. If I could have taken wing, I couldn't have felt a greater thrill. In that hour, I promised the sea my life.

After that, I slept like a house cat. My only dream was of being eight feet tall and knocking myself silly on the lintel as I stepped out of *my* cabin on *my* schooner, the *Allie*. Turned out just to be Phil Wood shaking me awake at seven bells.

Cook and I made duff for dinner again Monday. (No raisins—they were strictly a Sunday treat.) The molasses barrel had been drained to such a low level, I couldn't fill a pitcher from the spigot. "Take the lid off," Cook said, handing me a ladle. Then he went to take a nap, I supposed, in that sacred pantry of his.

Cook in the pantry, me busy stirring, and a lidless molasses barrel equaled too much temptation for Allie. Before I knew it, she'd hopped up on the barrel edge. Down into the barrel went an arm. Out came a finger coated with molasses.

Licking that finger was nice, so in it went again.

I couldn't stop stirring or the duff would scorch. "*Stop that!*" I hissed. I know Allie heard me, and understood me too! She grinned, stuck her paw in to above the wrist, and began to stir the molasses in imitation of the way I was stirring duff. All I needed was for Cook to emerge from the pantry and catch her at it. I shoved the duff off the heat and grabbed her.

Off came my shirt again. This time I wet it with some of the water Cook was heating for coffee.

Allie didn't enjoy having her paw scrubbed. With a quick twist, she was free and leaping. Wet, sticky shirt in hand, I went after her. Delighted that I was ready to stop that boring stirring and play with her, she backed out of my reach all the way to the wall. I lunged for her, but she was too quick for me. She shoved the pantry door open and skittered in. The door swung back toward me when I was halfway through it, banging my knee.

My gasp was not from the pain to my knee.

A lantern suspended from the low ceiling showed me Cook, sitting on an upended crate, holding a baby in his arms. The biggest cleaver on the *Newburyport Beauty* lay beside the crate, and as Cook's right arm shot toward it, I felt myself helplessly frozen.

May 1852

T he farmer's dogs sniff the dried blood on Ogun's legs through the bramble rips in his trousers. Ogun and his mother climb into the farmer's high-sided wagon and lie down side by side on its straw. Over them, the farmer and his son lower the wagon's false-bottomed top and begin to cover it: Yams, turnips, cabbages thump an inch above Ogun's nose. Lying in darkness, he keeps expecting one to break through and bash his face.

If he needed to sit up, he couldn't. He mustn't think about that. Mile after mile, he clenches his fists and sweats.

Now and then over the wagon's bumping and creaking, Ogun hears low words that he can't separate from each other. Both farmer and son are taking Ogun and his mother to wherever it is that they're going. Ogun wonders whether his mother is right to trust this pair. After his father ran away, the master posted a reward for his return. Probably now he's posted one for Ogun and his mother. Of course he has.

"How we know these buckra don' mean to turn us in?" Ogun murmurs.

"Hush your mouth, chile," his mother says, but her voice is strained.

Ogun has no way of knowing how long they've traveled or how far when a challenge stops the horse. "What you got there in that wagon, Grampaw?"

"Vegetables for the market," Ogun hears the farmer's cheerful answer. "The early cabbage catches the cash!"

"Let's just have a look, Gramps." The second voice is no friendlier than the first, and Ogun smells his sweat souring from the ordinary stink of overheated, unwashed boy to the acrid stench of terror. Can the challengers smell it too? There's a knothole in the false bottom above his eye. He shuts both eyes. His eyeball is help-lessly, hopelessly white, but maybe his eyelid is the color of the wagon's bottom. His chest is gripped in a vise of fear. He feels his mother's hand slide over his.

Chapter 12

Cook's Story

On its way to his deadly cleaver, Cook's hand paused momentarily, then picked up instead the knotted rag it had dropped. "Come in and let the door close," Cook said, "and sit down."

Once my legs would obey me, I obeyed Cook.

"This baby's name be Yemaya: my granddaughter."

I needed to start breathing.

"Her mother name this baby for goddess of the sea."

I felt pressure against the small of my back. Allie was making herself invisible to Cook, I'm sure she supposed. I pulled her around to where I could keep a firm grip on her.

"Now it be the sea that her mother be praying will free her." As Cook spoke, he continually dipped his rag into a cup of milk, then stuck the knot into the mouth of the baby in his lap. The baby sucked lustily.

"This baby *belong*"—Cook spoke the word so bitterly I shrank—"to same man who did own *me*. Until one day some people nail me in a coffin and load me on a train for Massachusetts." Cook paused and, for an instant, a half grin replaced his glare. "Field hand do fit in coffin easier than cook."

I was too stunned to smile. Was Cook a fugitive slave too? Did Uncle Thad realize what danger he was in? Of losing his vessel, of losing his livelihood, of prison? I didn't believe Uncle Thad would ever lie. Yet either he'd lied to me or he'd been grossly deceived. By Cook. My chest was so tight I didn't know if I could speak, but I managed. "We have got to tell my uncle. We've got to tell him, right away."

"Your uncle know, boy."

From scalp to toes, I turned cold. "But he told me—" I had to stop to swallow.

"He tole you what he had to tell you."

My words came out a whisper. "He lied to me."

"You think on every word. I doubt the captain lie."

I couldn't "think on every word." I couldn't think at all. "Deceived, then. My own uncle—"

"Deceive you for your protection, boy. What you don't know, you can't be blame for."

I was acutely conscious of the gentle clatter of the pots and ladles behind me on the galley wall, of the *Beauty's* slow pitch and roll under me, constants scarcely noticed after my first few days aboard. Now I understood why Cook slept in a hammock in the galley. I sat on the floor in front of him, my arms wrapped tightly around Allie. I dared not let her misbehave, with Cook so close to his cleaver. There wasn't much room for flight in that pantry, small to begin with and crowded with bags, boxes, and barrels. Though not so crowded as a coffin.

Maybe not so crowded as a prison cell.

Cook resumed his story as calmly as if I'd never interrupted. "When that Newburyport baggage master unload that box my coffin been in, he stand it on end. And he happen to stand it so I been *head down*. Those people meeting me afraid to come till dark. I stand on my head in that box all day! Time they let me out, corpse wouldn't have stunk no worse.

"I've worked for your uncle since that season. After I save enough, your daddy take my money to my old master down in South Carolina and buy my freedom and my wife, Cora's, too. Bring her back to me on the *Black Skimmer*." Cook smiled mischievously. "I wouldn't drown your daddy's monkey, boy."

So that's how my parents knew Cora! No wonder she was so patient with me when I was ill. But why hadn't Mam ever mentioned it? Unlike what Uncle Thad was doing, Father's actions had been perfectly legal. Not to mention just grand. Mam and her "flies don't enter shut mouths"! I wondered what else my parents weren't telling me.

"That leave my daughter." Cook's smile was gone. "My daughter, plus her husband, plus my grandson to save for. And then this child too. One night my daughter's husband run away. Run all the way to Canada. Sent my daughter word—*Come. Bring the children. Just get here, you be free. Don't have to pay for what belong to you already.* But my daughter, she been afraid to travel with this baby. Can keep her little boy quiet; can't keep baby quiet.

"Now this baby's father waiting for me to bring her to him. If my daughter and my grandson made it, they be waiting with him."

And if they didn't?

I tried to imagine me still a baby and Mam leaving me behind. I couldn't. But I couldn't imagine "belonging" to somebody else, either. "How did your daughter get the baby this far?"

"What you don't know, you can't tell."

The back of my neck tingled. "You think I'm going to blab?"

"I mean *I* don't know, so *I* can't tell, so if somebody do tell, everybody know it wasn't me."

Father likes to quote Benjamin Franklin's "Three may keep a secret, if two of them are dead." Uncle Thad, one; Cook, two; me, three. I glanced nervously at Cook's cleaver, then told myself not to be silly.

Then I told myself, not for the first time, to stay away from the *Beauty*'s railing after dark.

On the floor beside Cook was a large, open-topped

oval basket generously padded with rags. Gesturing with his head, Cook ordered me to examine it. "Feel in there. Tell what you find."

Allie'd been fidgeting. Now as I let go of her and rose, she scrambled up onto a potato sack farther from Cook.

My hand in the basket felt through the cloths to the basket bottom sooner than I'd expected.

"Take this chile."

I'd never been handed a baby before. I was sure it would scream, or I would drop it, or both. I stood stock-still. The baby just smiled.

Cook fiddled with the basket rim some and lifted. The basket had a lower compartment. "That where she lie when she come to me. This lady, she fill the top part with greens and bring her to me on deck like that. I pay her thirty cents for those greens, basket and all, in front of everybody." He didn't mention in what harbor.

He replaced the basket's top compartment, took back the baby, and laid her in it. Right away Allie jumped up on my shoulder. I think she wanted to remind me that I already had a pet.

"My wife, she want my daughter's family to

come live in Newburyport, in Guinea with her, but this law they got now chase that idea right off the yardarm!"

I knew what law he was talking about. The law that says even a penniless person who helps a runaway slave can be sent to jail for six months. The law that says if you're looking for runaway slaves, anybody you ask to help has to help, even the runaway's next-door neighbor. Even a preacher, even a law officer. ("Some law," Father fumes, "that requires a Massachusetts policeman to help people flout the laws of Massachusetts!")

"Everybody in Guinea know all about everybody else in Guinea," Cook said, "and know about rewards too. Guinea folk been poor. It's not just white folks who'll trash black folks for money." Cook sat back down on his crate; I sat on that potato sack of Allie's. "Now I worry about my wife. I leave her alone so much. Bounty hunters, they be crooked as angleworms. One might lay hands on her, swear she's a runaway, pretend he's come to take her back where she 'belong.' Take her down South and sell her, sell her like a mule. It be happening, since they got that law."

"But she has papers! You bought her freedom!"

"Paper burn easy, boy."

I was glad of Allie's warmth on my shoulder. "Hawk has a newspaper," I began.

"He show me."

So Hawk knew too! I thought again of Mr. Franklin's views on secrets. Why hadn't Hawk thrown that newspaper over the side?

"There isn't one person aboard who isn't entitled to be here," Uncle Thad had sworn. If he felt Yemaya was entitled to freedom, maybe that wasn't a lie. Phineas Ward would say it was, sure as thunder, but maybe God wouldn't.

Well, whether Uncle Thad had lied to me or not, he had to be warned about the man I'd seen on the dock at Salisbury watching who got on and off the *Beauty*. Making sure his prey didn't escape him, I figured. Uncle Thad had to be warned of that man fast. Taking a deep breath, I told Cook just enough.

Cook turned the color of a squash that's lain too long in the sun. "*Tell him,*" he rasped.

Allie and I were already out the pantry door.

May 1852

Ogun hears his mother weeping at night, when she thinks he's asleep. He figures she misses that baby. Ogun misses the extra rations his mother'd been getting because she was feeding that baby. She'd shared them with Ogun and his father. Until his father left. Right before Ogun's birthday.

Ogun doesn't miss that baby, but if his mother wants it, then Ogun wants her to have it. Where is it?

"I think you know!" he'd accused her. "How come you don' tell me?"

"Oh, son," she'd said, and her face had lost its smooth, closed look. "What iffen they was to catch us, and what iffen they was to say to you, 'You tell us where that chile is, or we hurt your ma'?"

So he was right, she knows where that baby is. Or maybe she doesn't. Maybe she just knows where it's supposed to be.

Chapter 13

Helpless

Uncle Thad didn't waste time on explanations or apologies. "We'll skip Hampton," he said. "Sail straight from Portsmouth to Grand Manan."

Canada's Grand Manan Island was where Cook's son-in-law was waiting. And Cook's daughter and grandson? No way of knowing whether they'd made it there too or not. "We'll skip Kennebunk and Portland also; serve them and Hampton on our way back down."

"What will the crew think?" I was shivering.

"Crews aren't paid to think. Crews are paid to take orders."

That sounded ugly, but then I remembered this: Slaves aren't paid to think, or to take orders either. Slaves aren't paid at all.

What else was ugly was that I had to accept, finally, what all this meant about Uncle Slye. "Is Uncle Slye really so jealous that he's willing to ruin you?" I asked.

Uncle Thad's face was a mask. "Ray," he said, "it's a wicked old world."

"Yes, sir," I said, and left him then, sitting there. I had the feeling he didn't want to talk.

Back in the steamy galley, I told Cook about Uncle Thad's new plans. Cook had already passed the crew's dinner through their sliding door, and we could hear the steady clinking of spoons. There's not much conversation when the crew eats. Neither did Cook speak, just sucked in his cheeks, nodded, and handed me Uncle Thad and Mate's tray.

Mate actually acknowledged receiving his grub. Mannerly wasn't Mate's middle name, but since I'd accepted that bowsprit assignment without trying to get Uncle Thad to let me out of it, he'd been noticeably civil.

Once this would have given me great satisfaction. Now I had bigger concerns than how I rated with Mate. The man on the dock was bad news, like that bird whose name sailors don't like to utter, that only alights on your vessel when it knows you're going to sink.

Where did Phineas Ward get his tip? Where did the man who gave it to him get it? Or—the thought was a bit slow coming—the *woman* who gave it to him? Probably, I considered, nobody other than Yemaya's mother knew how she'd been smuggled aboard the *Beauty*. No, Yemaya's mother and the woman who filled the top half of the basket with greens and handed the whole priceless package over to Cook, in public, for thirty cents. How much had Yemaya's mother paid her? Or was she a friend who did it for nothing? Was she the basket maker herself? Or was there another woman who knew what that bottom compartment was going to hold, one who didn't mind being paid once for making it and once more for telling somebody about it?

I thought I knew what Cook would answer if I speculated to him along these lines. "No use beatin' a dead horse," he'd said when I'd made an angry comment about his life before he escaped to Newburyport and the *Beauty*. Now we needed to set our minds to work, not our mouths. More than smells pass through the galley's warped bulkhead, and the crew was dining just on the other side of it.

When Allie and I got back from the captain's cabin, Cook had already filled his own bowl and mine. As he passed me mine, our eyes met and he nodded grimly. Then we both sat down. I could tell Cook could have been eating wet flour for all the pleasure his duff was giving him. I felt the same way, but one thing Father taught me before I even started school was that an empty stomach leaves room for fear. "Fill up your gut, Ray," I remember him saying when I didn't like squash for supper. "You don't want the terrors filling it for you."

I wouldn't want any of my classmates ever to suspect that I was scared of ghosts as a small boy. Father said that if you ate so much you fell asleep as your head hit the pillow, nary a ghost would come near you. Now, without knowing I was going to speak, I heard myself asking, "Have you ever been afraid of ghosts, Cook?"

"People run their mouths, right soon they have something to run from," Cook snapped, and sent me to milk Mandy.

But while Allie and I were gone, he started washing up the duff pot and the crew's kids. He'd never helped me clean up after dinner before, always sat in the pantry playing his banjo—to Yemaya of course, I realized now—or strolled out right past me with his pipe and a final warning about what would happen to me if I opened his pantry door. His Bluebeard's closet, I'd taken to calling it to myself.

Today, after I'd finished the washing and set the kids and things outside the galley door to drip-dry and Cook had fed Yemaya, Cook sat back down in the galley. Apparently he didn't feel like a smoke this afternoon. He planted his bench between Yemaya's door and the rest of the world, staring at the door to the deck as if it were an army of bounty hunters and he was ready to fight them all.

"Was the woman who sold you those greens a

friend?" I wanted to ask him. Or more directly: "Who could have tipped off Phineas Ward?" I swallowed a couple of times, reached up, and gave Allie a nervous scratch. "How does rice grow?" I asked instead. "I never have seen any growing in Massachusetts."

"Don't hold your breath till you do," said Cook. "Rice like *hot*. You moan and groan and whimper, think this galley been hot."

I did not moan *or* whimper, but when we had a pot or two boiling and the oven fired up, anybody who could read minds would have read me groaning, sure enough, so I let Cook talk.

"Rice grow in them field between them river, where use to be swamp," he said. "River and swamp water go up when ocean go up and down when ocean go down, four foot—six foot some of 'em— two time every day. Before my time, Guinea men build all them dam, dig all them trench four foot deep. Put in them gate that lift up or drop down, tell river when it can come in them swamp and when it must stay out, so them swamp can all be rice field. Them gate—they call 'em 'trunks'—them trunks tell them rice field, *Now you can be water,* and then, *Now you got to drain and let them rice seed get planted,* and then, *Now you got to be water again so them rice bird don't eat all the seed.*"

I'd heard Cora call our bobolinks rice birds, though I'd never asked her why. (Cora set Mam back, telling her what good eating Mam's beloved bobolinks were.)

"Then them trunks say, *Drain,*" Cook went on, "*so sun make that rice grow,* and then, *Let in some water so trash float up so man can gather it and throw it out.*

"Come summer, rice field got to be hoed. Drain them field and hoe and flood again and drain and hoe and flood again and drain and hoe, and it so hot you think your eye going to cook like a boil egg. Keep checking that rice. When rice begin to joint, it been harvest time. Ox take that rice to the mill.

"Come frost, time to clean this year's stubble out of them rice field. That stubble been so thick you can't plow it under, have to burn it. Then you can tell the trunk, *Come high tide, lift up, let that water back in.* All winter them rice field going to be swamp again.

"February, come low tide, trunk door let that water out, and you got to come with hoe and turn mud. Water been cold, and mud stink. Even in February, mud stink worse than hog fart. Driver tell you how much mud you got to turn today before you can go home.

"You don't know what a driver be, do you boy?" Cook interrupted his story to challenge, not unkindly.

I knew he would tell me whether I answered or not, so I just stroked Allie's tail, which she'd looped halfway around my neck, and looked interested.

"A driver not been any freer than his neighbors," Cook went on lecturing, with scarcely a pause to swallow spit. "But he the one make sure the Street quiet down at night, call his neighbors out to work in the morning, get 'em on barges to take 'em to rice fields by sunrise. And he tell everybody his task that day. Overseer got thirty mile of rice land to see over—he can't watch *your* field all the time. Got a whole plantation to oversee. Got to have somebody to pass on his orders, make sure they get minded. Overseer tell drivers, 'Say to each man how much mud he must turn today.' If driver want something you got and you won't give it to him, he give you more task than you can do and then he beat you because you didn't do it. Driver can tie you down and beat you till you bleed. If overseer come by, he take driver's word. Don't nobody make driver no trouble."

One of Mam's brothers is an overseer on a cotton plantation in Texas. He visited us last Christmas; it was the first time we'd met since I was a toddler. I admit I was all full of myself, wanted to show him how much I'd grown up. I asked him, "If the slaves on that plantation are happy, what do the owners need a Fugitive Slave Law for?" I thought it was a good question, but that minute Mam sent me to the basement for a jug of cider, and when I got back, everybody was talking about various kinds of apples. And Mam lectured me at bedtime about the manners expected of a host.

Cook had paused, and I sensed that he was about to turn away from *his* lecture for a bit, that a story was coming, but he frowned, looked away a couple of seconds, and got back to educating me.

"If you got to dig more new trench, you take a hoe blade big as my foot and dig you a trench in the mud wide as my hand. Finish one trench, dig another beside it. And another. And another. One quarter acre got eighty-four trench. Dig all them trench, leave 'em for the women to plant."

Briefly I pictured Cook and the other men lying back in the shade while their wives did the work, but Cook hadn't finished. "Go with them other men to high ground, plant all *them* acre. Plant rye, corn, collard greens—all such thing, while them women plant rice. All March, half April, women drop rice seed in trench, scrape that rotten-smelling mud over it with they foot so it won't float away when that trunk gate let that water in. Bless God, my wife, Cora, work in the weaving room, never had to plant rice.

"'Long about second week in April, women stop right where they at. That trunk door get lifted, water creep in till all that seed been covered so rice bird can't see it. No more rice planting till June, on account of rice bird. Them bird, they fly up north every June, want to fill up for the trip first, fill up on rice seed! In June after rice bird gone, women drop in some more seed. Two bushel every acre, every seed dropped by hand, covered up by foot.

"All the time, every day hotter. May we kept going by singing. June, couldn't spare the breath. June we kept gon' with prayers to sweet Jesus; no sound, just between us and Jesus. *Jesus, get me to the end of this row. Of this day. Of this life.*

"Come a day when our carpenter see he gon' need more nails. Carpenter been too important to quit his work and row to Charleston. I beg him, 'Tell Overseer send me. I got boat, tell 'im.' Night before, I done took my boat, caught my wife, Cora, some fish. Come home just about sundown, see a driver steal a ham from the smokehouse. And he see me.

"I wasn't gon' crack my teeth about that ham, but the task that driver set me in the morning been twice what any other man in the field get set. But when Carpenter need nails and tell Overseer I got boat, Overseer call for me. Overseer didn't ever think I'd run off and leave my wife, my daughter, her son. He didn't know about that ham.

"Overseer didn't give me money, just a piece of

paper he wrote on. 'You give that store man this paper, bring me the nails he give you.' But when I got to Charleston, I took my courage in my two hand."

I sat a little straighter; this lecture was going to get exciting. But Cook, who all this while had been watching me keenly as if to be sure I understood him, abruptly looked away. "You don't need to know what come next," he said. "All them people who help me still in Charleston."

"Did you ride all the way from South Carolina in that coffin?" I asked quickly. Surely I could get him started again. But Cook heard a noise from the pantry and stood up. "Time you learned you a new skill," he said, and pointedly held the pantry door open for me.

I hadn't heard anything.

I preceded Cook into the pantry. "Sit," he said, and once I sat, he put that Yemaya in my lap. Allie must have read his mind, for the second I sat down and Cook turned my way, she jumped off my shoulder and hastened to hide behind a biscuit barrel.

Cook meant me to feed Yemaya, but to my

relief, he'd fed her so recently himself that we couldn't wake her up enough. She was *not* interested. I think Allie was glad when Cook said he guessed it was time I reported to Mate, even though she'd never thought highly of Mate before.

I, of course, preferred listening to Cook talk. Cora hadn't been a rice planter; Cook was pleased about that. What about his mother? Had she worked in the weaving room too? But what if she hadn't—what if she'd had to sow rice every single March in cold, stinking mud?

"Did your mother ever tell you you were too short?" I asked Cook while he settled Yemaya back in her basket.

Cook cut his eye at me, then walked right past me, headed back into the kitchen. Allie and I followed. "My ma stood me against the wall beside the stove every birthday," Cook said. "Cut a little line with a kitchen knife to show how high top of my head come to. From time I been six to time I been fifteen, them little marks didn't hardly part with one another. Year I been sixteen, that mark leap up like flame in the fireplace. My ma say, 'Boy, you better quit eatin' before you bump your head on the moon.'" Smiling to himself, Cook reached for his smallest skillet. "Now, git along with you."

Come night, the wind was from the north. We beat our way up the coast. Moonlight flittered on the water, and some other time I would have thought this beautiful. Now I thought only of my flittering innards. Some other time I would have described our unloading in Portsmouth Tuesday morning as brisk, but now that I knew about Yemaya, I was a lot more demanding. The sooner we got under way, the safer we were from bounty hunters. Earlier I'd imagined telling Tom Chase about something in Portsmouth that was grander than anything in Newburyport; there must be something. But I didn't put a foot over the side at Portsmouth, and watching others do so put a cramp in my stomach. Cook had to go ashore, of course, to grub up. Every other crew member walking down the gangplank seemed a threat. How many besides Hawk knew everything I knew about the *Beauty*'s cargo?

I could not get what Benjamin Franklin said off my mind.

May 1852

Every year on his birthday, Ogun's mother has marked his height on the cabin wall. If they were to go back now, this year's mark would be lower than last year's, Ogun thinks. Surely he's walked at least an inch off his feet since he snatched up his slingshot and crept out the cabin door. His feet and his shoes, Ogun figures, had a bet going, which would give up first. Shoes have lost. Ogun hides what's left of them under a matted tangle of honeysuckle.

In no time, a thorn finds his left foot. Already there's too little light to search for it. Ogun limps along beside his mother, trying to walk so that she won't notice. An owl's call quavers somewhere near, and his mother grips his hand. Ogun reminds himself that his mother calls him Little Owl, but the quavery hoot makes his shoulders swallow his neck like a turtle shell.

Supperless, they stop for the night at last beside a

cornfield, waking in the morning too soon to be rested but not too soon to be ravenous. Ogun tears the nearest cob from its stalk, rips the husk away from its juicy kernels, starts swallowing saliva before he can even get the cob to his teeth. His mother works one row over. Crows fly up, denouncing them, and they both shrink, fearing that someone with a gun must surely notice the clamor, but no one comes. By Ogun's count, it's Sunday. That's probably why.

For once Ogun would rather be in church than where he is. Ogun isn't much for sermons, though he's outgrown being too scared by them to go to sleep Sunday nights. Like that one on God asking Isaac's father to cut Isaac's throat. Nothing in Ogun's life led him to think that any angel would make a special trip to rescue *him*, but his mother'd taken care of that worry.

"You safe," she'd said grimly. "I's here. God knowed better than to ask Sarah."

Chapter 14

Unwelcome Lesson

I didn't let myself think that any of Cook's shipmates would betray him to the Portsmouth authorities just for reward money. I told myself that it was in the interest of every man aboard to protect Uncle Thad. If he were fined and jailed, the *Beauty* would have to be sold, and the crew would all be looking for jobs. And I argued to myself that if any of the *Beauty*'s hands were going to betray Cook, well, they'd all had plenty of chances before now.

Myself argued back that if a man was a little worried to start with, that worry could grow bigger and bigger until finally it was too big to squash. Six months in jail is no joke if your family's got nobody else to support it. Uncle Thad's in-laws would take care of Aunt Edith and my cousins, but what about Phil Wood or the Plumers? Could they count on their neighbors to look after their wives and children?

Of course it was Mate who really troubled me. Not just what he'd said about Mr. Garrison and his abolitionists, but that threat about throwing overboard any black stowaways I'd heard him make to Hawk. Thinking of that, my mind slapped me with a vision of a wailing baby hitting the waves, and my knees seemed to dissolve.

And the more I worried, the more I raked up to worry about. Recalling Mate's anger at Mr. Garrison and his abolitionist friends brought back an ordinary memory, which now seemed a little less ordinary.

I'd sensed that my parents didn't care for the

Fugitive Slave Law, though they didn't say much about it. Now, remembering how serious Mam had been about my mouthing off to Clam in support of abolitionists, I began to feel a bit uneasy. Bostonians should clear their city of abolitionists, Clam Hopkins had declared, and I'd suggested a welcome for any such exiles in Newburyport. Mam had been displeased. Could Mam and Father know what Uncle Thad was doing? If Uncle Thad got caught, could they go to jail too?

What in this world would Father do if he lost the *Black Skimmer*?

As Cook had stepped onto the gangplank, I had warned Allie that I was going to run one quick errand to the hold without her and then, except for when I visited Mandy with my pail and Yemaya with my cup, she and I were staying in the galley till he got back. Mate or anybody else trying to take Yemaya out of that pantry would do it over my dead body. "And you," I told her, "are to bite him."

She looked willing.

More willing to bite somebody than I figured she'd be to cooperate if I tried to feed Yemaya, as I was terrified I was going to have to do before Cook got back. I prepared for the worst. First, I would need a bribe to pacify Allie. In the dark hold, I said a silent anti-spiders prayer nonstop as I broke off the first banana I could reach and climbed out of there. Right then was a bad time for me to die in agonized contortions. Who would protect Yemaya if Phineas Ward came looking for her while Uncle Thad and Cook and Hawk were all ashore?

I put Allie's banana inside my shirt where she couldn't get at it and returned to the galley.

Yemaya didn't reproach me for my brief absence, just sucked away on that knotted rag of hers. And no wonder. Cook had tied some sugar inside the knot.

Next, to give myself a way to account for the hours I'd spent in the galley while everybody else was ashore, I peeled potatoes. I peeled enough potatoes to last us if we sailed to the North Pole. I also knotted my own handkerchief around a lump of sugar and put it back in my pocket. Just in case.

But I wasn't virtuously peeling potatoes when Cook got back. Yemaya had begun to fuss at last. When I reminded her of the sugar-lump rag, she pushed it away. She wasn't going to be fobbed off with any such pawky substitute for FOOD. I was getting panicky. Allie, stubborn and mischievous and jealous and contrary as usual, was keeping neatly out of reach. Why hadn't I been prepared for this; why hadn't I tethered Allie before Yemaya woke up? Waving the banana at Allie seemed to confirm her suspicions of me, and she skittered even farther away. I bit off a piece of the banana and made a show of mashing it in my mouth, hoping to lure her within easy grabbing distance.

No takers.

I put a piece of banana into Yemaya's mouth, making sure Allie saw me. I could do that without picking Yemaya up. Was she old enough to be given banana? I prayed that the answer was yes, but it didn't matter, because she wouldn't even hold it in her mouth three seconds. Out it smershed. As she screwed up her face, she took a breath and her shoulders rose—I knew a real blast was coming. It was heaven's blessing that the crew were all ashore, but who knew when somebody might come thumping back aboard?

I don't know any lullabies. I couldn't pick Yemaya up and rock her the way I'd seen Cook do without the risk that my jealous monkey would start destroying things, and me not able to stop her fast. I had to drown out Yemaya somehow, and I can't play the banjo. Cook walked back in on me singing "Haul on the Bowline" loud enough to carry to the bridge, or pretty near.

I wondered if he'd think I'd lost my mind, but when my voice broke, his grin was friendly.

And I got another lesson in Yemaya feeding. With Cook on hand, Allie wasn't about to interfere. I silently vowed I'd finish off that banana myself, right in front of her.

Yemaya must be five times as heavy as Allie. She wasn't half as much fun to feed. Allie lets you know how much she enjoys her food. That bony little pink face positively radiates pleasure. Yemaya just lay in my lap with her eyes tight shut, sucking and sucking, and how I knew she'd had enough was she let the rag fall out of her mouth and her eyes unsquinched. Not opened, just unsquinched. Yemaya didn't go in for *thank you* noises like Allie.

I'd have thought Cook would let well enough alone when she dropped off like that, but blessed if he didn't take that sleepy baby out of my lap, hold her with her head sort of on his shoulder, and start thumping her back. He kept that up till she made a noise like a bullfrog.

"Got to do that every time, or you just throwing milk away," Cook assured me as he laid Yemaya in her bed.

Freeing me to get back to worrying about squealers and bounty hunters.

And soon another worry was added to these. By dinnertime, our Portsmouth trading was done, the crew all back aboard, but the *Beauty* sat where she was, moored in the harbor with several other vessels awaiting a wind. We needed to fly, and we couldn't even stir. The crew scraped their kids of potato hash clean. I hoped this meant clean consciences.

Right after dinner, Allie and I took our pail to Mandy, who, as ever in good weather, was tethered to the mainmast. Allie, who always needs a nap after she eats, made herself a bed in Mandy's hay. Me, I was fidgety as a half-hatched chick; I couldn't have slept if you'd hit me over the head with a rolling pin. We needed to sail!

Mate was swaggering around the quarterdeck,

yelling at the crew. Afloat, the captain doesn't have to raise his voice. I'd never heard Uncle Thad give an order since I'd come aboard. Uncle Thad gave his instructions quietly to Mate, and Mate did the shouting.

Uncle Thad was on the quarterdeck too, scanning the harbor with the four-foot spyglass Grandfather bought in Rotterdam. I knew the barrel shape he was looking for. I'd given him a good description of Phineas Ward.

I wondered if his mouth was dry as cotton like mine.

I milked "about a cupful." As I straightened up, I noticed Cook leave the galley. For the head, I supposed. I also noticed Uncle Thad cross to the rail, raise his spyglass again, and apparently focus on something between the *Beauty* and the docks.

In seconds, Mate was staring in the same direction as Uncle Thad. That was enough to make me forget about delivering Mandy's milk. I nudged Allie awake, patted my shoulder for her to hop back up, then hurried to the side myself and peered in the same direction as Uncle Thad and Mate on the quarterdeck.

A longboat with two stout oarsmen and two passengers was threading its way through the other vessels at anchor, maybe headed for us. We were anchored, our sails furled, with neither wind nor tide ready to take us away. If guests should arrive at our side, we had no way to avoid them.

I tried telling myself that if the longboat were indeed coming to us, it was just bringing messengers from another vessel. Some other captain was inviting Uncle Thad to supper. "The wicked flee when no man pursueth," Mam says when I swear I didn't break something before she's even asked. But I had a cold feeling.

Mate came down the quarterdeck ladder and tramped past me without a glance. When I saw he was heading for the galley, I raced to snatch up my pail again and try to at least overtake him.

And I started to pray. Cook, I saw, was just on his way back from the head. Mate was going to beat us both to the galley. In he'd barge, barking for Cook as he stepped through the door. And sure as Satan, Yemaya would respond.

I was trotting so fast I was leaving a trail of sploshed milk, and Allie's complaints were shrill in my ear. I saw the moment Cook noticed Mate, saw his head jerk back, his stride quicken. Mate didn't notice Cook. Now I was slopping milk like Hansel dropping pebbles, but Mate still beat me to the galley door.

Not by much. As he laid a hand on it, I took a sharp breath and dumped the rest of Mandy's milk on his heels.

"Oh!" I cried. "I'm sorry! I tripped!"

Mate was roaring like a shot bear, but Cook caught up with us before I got smashed. And Mate remembered what his captain had sent him to say: Cook to the quarterdeck at once.

Hurrying to beat Mate to the galley, Cook must have seen that longboat too, for his face was the color of dead leaves, and his response to Mate's order was to freeze. I eased around the two of them to stand between Mate and the galley entrance.

I could've kicked 'em both in the shins, and neither'd have noticed.

Cook didn't move. Mate's whole face turned the color of his freckles.

I bet Uncle Thad hadn't actually told Mate to say "at once." He knew that under these circumstances, Cook would need a little time. If Uncle Thad could've sent Hawk for Cook instead of Mate, Cook could just have said, "Wait while I try to make things safe as I can!" and Hawk would've made haste to help him. But relayed by Mate, Uncle Thad's orders had become *right-now-at-once-immediately*. All Cook could do was turn a stricken face to me and say, "Ray. *See to things!*" as Mate hustled him away.

"I will," I called after him. I ducked into the galley as fast as I could move without dumping Allie. My stomach had knotted to the size of an apple. *Things!* didn't mean supper, except to Mate.

May 1852

I t is May. On the plantation, time for everybody to get new shoes. A pair in November, another pair in May. When they find Ogun's father, will he be able to give Ogun shoes? The scraps of Ogun's last November pair are rotting in a honeysuckle thicket that Ogun never expects to see again. And wouldn't recognize if he did. At home—

Ogun considers that he can go right on thinking of the cabin as home until his father builds them a new one. Just not out loud. Just not to his mother, who says, "That place not home. Freedom our home now."

At home, a month and more ago, Ogun had set his foot down on an inch-wide strip of wood and held still while his mother marked this strip to show how long his foot was. Then his father, grumbling, had cut the strip's end off at that mark. Everybody on the Street was doing this job. These strips got handed to the overseer, who wrote each person's name on his "measure" with a dark pencil. Each measure got sent along to Charleston to be matched with a new pair of shoes.

Sometimes the shoes Ogun got were too narrow, but usually they were too wide. "Give you room to grow," his mother told him.

Last November the master had stood on a platform, smiling at everybody, first day for grown-ups, next day for children. Each man's name was read out for him to step up, scrape his foot, bob his head, and thank the master for giving him his red flannels, his rolls of homespun, his new hat and shoes. Briefly, Ogun had feared that he wasn't going to get to take part in this ceremony, wasn't going to get *any* shoes, tight or loose, or any of the rest of his winter rations either.

Grown-ups as usual had gone up on the platform the first day, and the children had watched, seen once again how to behave when it was their turn. But the minute the master had set out for the Big House the first evening, Ogun's father had tramped up his cabin steps, stamped into the cabin, and slammed the door behind him. He'd dropped his dress goods on the floor, given them a kick, and flung his new shoes across the room. "Today been the last time I scrape my foot to the buckra for what I have earned," he vowed. "This been the last time, the last time I duck my head to that—"

Ogun didn't get to hear that *what*, for his mother had shushed his father and sent Ogun out to look for nuts in the woods. "I don't want to see you till this sack been full," she'd told him, almost pushing him out onto the porch.

Ogun picked up hickory nuts and black walnuts until the autumn light began to fade. He'd have filled his sack faster if he hadn't resolved to leave all acorns for the hogs that ranged the woods, free till butchering time. Nobody bought hog food or shoveled hog manure. Hogs ranged free, and when you needed a ham, you killed one. Ogun's family didn't own any hogs, just chickens. Ogun was leaving the acorns for the hogs as a charm. His May shoes already had been a little tight to begin with, and he was feeling their tightness all the more for the painful fear that his father might not let him go up on the platform in the morning and receive the master's gift of a new pair.

The charm had worked. Next day his father had worn his new shoes to work on a damaged dike, and Ogun had bowed and scraped and received the clothes he is wearing now.

That was last fall. Before the spring clothes giving, his father was gone.

And so was Ogun. And so was that last pair of initially loose, gradually tight shoes that the master had expected to last till May. The master wasn't figuring on Ogun walking to freedom.

Freedom had turned out to be farther than a pair of shoes away.

Chapter 15

Crisis

As I watched Mate all but drag Cook away, I prayed there'd be time for the plan my mind was frantically working on. I thunked the empty milk pail in the sink, yanked that handkerchief knotted around a sugar lump out of my pocket, swiped it across the pail's milky bottom. Then I headed aft as fast as I could without losing Allie. Allie scolded loudly, right into my ear. She does not like to be jounced around just after she eats.

At the quarterdeck rail, Uncle Thad, Mate, and Cook stared in the direction of that longboat. Nobody looked down to see Allie and me barge into Uncle Thad's cabin under their feet.

The medicine kit was locked.

Why hadn't I thought of that? Given what Uncle Thad had said about the mate who stole all the laudanum on his ship, of course the medicine kit was locked.

Laudanum takes time to work. "Fifteen minutes, Harriet," Dr. Spofford told Mam that time I fell out of the famous Newbury Elm. "At least." Right now I didn't know if I had fifteen minutes. I didn't have time to look for the key. I took the iron paperweight off Uncle Thad's desk and smashed the lock.

Three drops of laudanum went on the knotted lump that held the sugar in my milky handkerchief. Ignoring Allie's protests—more jouncing!—I raced back to the galley. Fear had me convinced that our approaching guests were after Yemaya.

All eyes were glued to the oncoming boat. Nobody paid any attention to me.

In the pantry, I set Allie down on her familiar

potato sack. Then I lit the hanging lamp so I could shut the swinging door to the galley behind us and still see.

It's been years since I broke my arm, but my tongue still starts cleaning itself every time I think of how bitter the laudanum Dr. Spofford gave me was. With my most desperate prayer of all, I smeared molasses on my knotted handkerchief, traded it to Yemaya for her sugary one, and held my breath.

Yemaya blinked, smiled, and got back to sucking.

I couldn't count on her to be equally agreeable if I took her and her bedding out of the basket top and laid her on the floor. And if it made her yell, there was no Cook to drown her out with his banjo. I shoved a sack of onions aside and set the basket top with Yemaya in it on the floor. Then I lifted Yemaya, bedding and all, into the basket's bottom. She just gurgled.

Now I began to pray nonstop—*don't let her cry, don't let her yell, don't let her fuss*—as I put the top section of the basket back in place.

Yemaya was used to the dark. She didn't even whimper.

And that scared me. It was what I wanted, what I needed, what I'd prayed for, but it scared me. There'd been nobody to ask how much laudanum was safe to give her. "Harriet," I will never forget hearing Dr. Spofford say to Mam, "I'm leaving you this bottle. After Ray wakens from what I just gave him, if the pain gets too much for him, you can give him one eyedropper's worth. One, no more, and not any sooner than in four hours, no matter how he carries on. People have died of too much laudanum."

"I'd rather this chile die," Cook had said to me once, "than be the reason her mother and brother get dragged back South. Better she die than grow up a slave." Maybe he thought he meant it, I figured. But just let him find her dead, just let him find *I'd* killed her, and everybody (including Cook) might discover how he really felt. I said a prayer and opened the galley door so I'd have light after I put out the lantern. As I took the lantern down and hid it behind some crates, two bells rang. So far, my exercise hadn't taken more than twenty minutes. But I wasn't done. What was I to put in the basket top?

Bananas, what else? The *Beauty*'s hold was full of them. Soon my arms were too. Allie got one, to bribe her to sit quietly just outside the galley door while I put the rest of my load in the top half of Yemaya's basket, then hurried back for a second load. Allie seemed to feel she was entitled to one from that trip too, but I ignored her.

I pulled the open molasses barrel and some crates in front of the door to the pantry and joined Allie just outside the galley.

What I saw then was exactly what I'd been fearing, but it was a punch to my gut anyhow.

Standing on the afterdeck where he'd just climbed aboard, red-faced, panting, was a figure out of my nightmares. Phineas Ward, bounty hunter. At his elbow, a constable. No more maybes.

I grabbed a tray, slammed a mug on it, collected Allie, and forced my legs to carry me closer to the last people on earth I wanted to see.

The constable had a droopy, rust-colored mustache and even more freckles than Mate: freckles on his eyelids, his lips. One more freckle, and he'd have had to put it in his pocket. He seemed to be pondering our deck polish. Phineas Ward's eyes darted all over the *Beauty* faster than Allie stealing pie.

Uncle Thad and Cook were standing side by side on the quarterdeck. Cook's right hand gripped papers. Uncle Thad's was in his big pocket. I stiffened, guessing what else was in that pocket.

Mate stepped up smartly to greet our visitors. "Captain's compliments; will you gentlemen take brandy with him in his cabin?"

The constable didn't lift his eyes from the deck.

"We have reliable information," stated Phineas Ward, "that you have stolen goods aboard. We mean to return them to their rightful owner. You will interfere at your peril."

Mate's face turned the color of the peeled potatoes I'd spent the morning piling up. *His* freckles stood out like smallpox.

"Aye, I'll visit him in his cabin," Ward continued. "I'll visit every inch of this ship if I have to. Then I'll visit him in jail."

The ignoramus didn't know a schooner from a ship. Maybe there were better places to have hidden Yemaya. Places Ignoramus Ward didn't know existed.

Too late now.

The constable didn't seem pleased by Ward's answer. Maybe that was my wishful thinking. Or maybe it was just his droopy mustache.

"To start with," Ward demanded, "what's *this?*"

It took me a second to realize that by "this," Ward meant Cook.

Cook knew. He held his papers closer—with both hands now.

Uncle Thad's hand stayed in his pocket. "*He* is my employee of many years, a free resident of Newburyport, Massachusetts. And there will be no papers ripped and tossed overboard today, gentlemen.

"We will not interfere with your search, but I assure you, your time would be better spent drinking my brandy than searching for stolen goods on my vessel."

Ward raised his voice. "Stand where you are, every man of you!"

Hawk, just alit from the foremast and headed aft, never broke stride. Phil Wood, replacing some worn chafing gear, shifted his tobacco quid from port to starboard, but he never looked up. The

Plumers, till now all eyes and ears, were suddenly absorbed by their work at the spun-yarn winch.

"I give the orders on this vessel," Uncle Thad said.

"Do your duty!" Ward snarled at the constable. "Do your duty, devil choke you, or I'll have you in court!"

"It's best not to interfere with the managing of a vessel, sir," the constable murmured, "unless you can swim."

My hopes grew that maybe the constable was on our side. The law required him to help this bounty hunter. That didn't mean he wanted to.

Ward turned abruptly away from him. "Stem to stern. Starting with his majesty's throne room."

Uncle Thad bowed and came down the ladder to open his cabin door for the guests himself. I wondered if they'd search even the hold. I wondered if anyone would tell them about banana spiders—one bite and you're carried ashore. I couldn't afford to stand around gawking, though. Quietly, trying to look calmly innocent, I took Allie and my camouflaging tray back in the galley.

There I began to chop garlic, one clove after

another. I wanted a stench so thick it would knock a man down as he stuck his head into the room. So thick he would maybe flee without even getting all the way in. So thick a banana spider would seem preferable. Now that it was too late, I'd lost all confidence in my plan. I kept praying for Cook to return and have a better idea.

Never a breath of him. I was on my own.

Too soon, I heard heavy footsteps. I braced myself. I would *not* throw myself in front of the pantry door, revealing to anybody with a wit in his head that the pantry contained something I wanted to stay hidden. I *would* keep my mouth shut, whatever happened, unless directly questioned. A guilty voice can say as much as words. I silently repeated and repeated these admonitions to myself while I chopped.

But the wild-eyed man who threw open the galley door wasn't Ward or the constable—it was Mate.

"Where is he?" Trying to shout quietly made Mate's voice hoarse.

I was so startled, my arms flew up and my knife went skittering across the floor. "He," I guessed, was the stowaway Mate had concluded Cook must be hiding. "Try the hold!" I cried. Then, as Mate seemed to hesitate, "Cook's all the time going down there, and when do we have bananas? Hurry!"

Mate turned without another word. I shut the door after him and took my knife away from Allie, who had pounced on it. And I prayed. "You must never lie, Ray," my father told me when I was small, "but you don't have to tell all you know."

My heart hadn't even stopped pounding yet when my next guests arrived.

June 1852

O gun was hungry. How many hours had he and his mother been walking with this stranger who called himself a friend? "Friends," according to the couple who'd hidden Ogun and his mother in their woodshed overnight, were what Quakers called themselves. All Quakers were opposed to slavery, the couple said. Ogun and his mother could trust this man. But how many hours had the three of them been walking, without ever laying eyes on another human being? How long since there'd been any sign that another human being had ever stepped where they were walking?

The name of this endless swamp was Dismal, their guide said. "Dismal" was a new word to Ogun and one that he was sure, if he lived to escape this place, he would never forget.

A skeleton-thin bird flew protesting from one cypress tree to another as half a dozen of the hairiest hogs Ogun had ever laid eyes on dashed grunting out of the brush and across his path. The beasts were long and lean as lizards, but a lot noisier. And smellier. Ogun's hand moved into his pocket, fingered his ammunition. A hog, he pointed out to his hand, is not a squirrel. Don't be silly.

The hogs ran single-mindedly, as if humans weren't worth a blink, and disappeared into the brush. That was when Ogun realized he'd been hearing steady chopping for some seconds and turned to see if his mother and the guide had heard it too. The guide was gone.

Ogun felt his bones turn to sand. Speechless, he looked in every direction. There was only his mother and the forest.

"As soon as we reach the lumber camp, I will leave thee," the guide had told them, but Ogun hadn't supposed that "as soon" meant so abruptly. How could the man know that they were hearing the axes of the very camp he had in mind? Who knew what Ogun and his mother were walking into? Could they be sure there'd be no white overseer in this camp, only slaves who would help them? Maybe this guide was no friend at all. Maybe he had a partner in this camp just waiting to be presented with two people he could turn in for money.

While Ogun worried, his mother continued her steady advance on the lumberers, and Ogun forced himself to keep up with her.

They stepped into a clearing whose size surprised Ogun. Tree felling must have been going on for days here. One tent, four mules, half a dozen men, all black. Ogun felt his gut relax a notch. The men stopped chopping to regard the two arrivals. They seemed interested rather than surprised. One propped his ax against his victim, a venerable cypress tree, and started toward Ogun and his mother. She had stopped walking once she'd been seen. The other men got back to work.

Suddenly some barking off in the woods that Ogun had scarcely been aware of changed to frantic, high-pitched yelps. Seconds later, a mongrel feist tore into the clearing, pursued by the ugliest sow Ogun had ever seen. His hands moved on their own, and a stone whizzed straight into the sow's right eye.

Almost as astonished as Ogun, the sow skidded to a stop, squealing like a hurricane. The little dog disappeared into the tent.

Now five more axes leaned against trees as their open-mouthed users took another look at Ogun. Ogun decided not to mention that he hadn't particularly aimed for that eye. Just for that sow. Which was now out of sight but not out of hearing, wildly lamenting her luck, retreating deeper into the swamp.

Work was forgotten as the men examined Ogun's slingshot, his remaining stones, his callused shooting fingers. Their praise, their admiring questions were all for Ogun, but they cut their eyes at his mother every half minute. Ogun gave short answers, expressionless for all their smiles. "A Friend will send for thee," that guide had told him and his mother, "as soon as he's filled his packet downriver." Ogun hoped this packet-filling friend's messenger would come soon.

"Thou wilt take this packet to New York," the guide had continued.

Ogun hadn't needed too very long to realize that "thou" was not some third party but his mother herself.

One of the buckras' strange ways of speaking, like Youboy. But he was still speculating about this packet's contents. Papers that said he and his mother were legally free had been his best guess. But how were they to get these papers to New York?

"The packet's name is the *Elizabeth Fry,*" the guide had said, and that made no sense to Ogun at all.

The loggers' driver knew the man who had guided Ogun and his mother. As the guide had promised, they were expected. The driver also knew the packet's captain. This "packet," it seemed, was a vessel, come south for her regular load of vegetables. Ogun and his mother were going to sail north to New York. Ogun hoped his astonished relief didn't show.

"Maybe you might cook for us till that captain send for you?" the driver said to Ogun's mother, with the biggest smile yet.

Soon, Ogun prayed. *Let this captain's messenger come soon.*

Chapter 16

Ward Pounces

Once the two hunters entered the galley, I realized that my garlic chopping had been time wasted. Ward's hair oil stank so, any skunk he approached would have held its breath while it ran to jump overboard. As for the constable, the law was requiring him to be close by Ward's side. Neither man was going to notice a little thing like air so thick with garlic I could have cut it with one of those eyelash-defying knives of Cook's.

"Stand back," ordered Phineas Ward. The constable, I flinched to see, had helped himself to the captain's cabin lantern. I had taken such care to hide the pantry lantern. The constable set the light on the galley floor, and he and Ward proceeded to open every cabinet. They checked every barrel for air holes. They opened every box big enough to house a possum.

Allie found the whole exercise wonderfully exciting; her toenails bit into my shoulder.

I'd stacked crates and the open molasses barrel in front of the pantry door. Now every crate was first opened and inspected, then set aside so the hunters could get at the next. At last this exposed the door.

"Ahh," sighed Ward. His nostrils dilated, and I swear he swelled even bigger. "Where does *this* little door go?"

"That just goes to the pantry, sir. You won't find anything you want in there."

He shot me a scornful look, which stretched into the nastiest triumphant smile I've ever seen outside of a bad dream. He shoved the molasses barrel out of the way and pushed on the door. Between my thighs I felt my new duck pants getting wet. It was strange to feel grateful that both men's eyes were fixed on the pantry.

I was sick with fear and self-reproach. All Yemaya had to do was wake up and whimper—not even wake up, just fart—and all would be over for her and Uncle Thad both. Why hadn't I talked over some kind of plan with Cook? What if he came charging down to put himself between these hounds and his precious grandchild? I'd been shocked by his "better she die than grow up a slave." From what I'd seen since, he might well have gone on to say "better *I* be dead." If these bloodhounds laid hands on that baby, he might do anything.

Since I'd taken down the hanging lantern, the pantry was dark as a pocket.

"Light," Ward demanded, and the constable stepped forward with Uncle Thad's lantern.

"Stand back and hold that lantern high," Ward ordered.

It took Ward a couple of moments to choose where to begin, I guess, but it didn't take Allie *one*.

She was down from my shoulder, heading for that basketful of bananas as the first lantern ray struck it. And as she darted between Ward and the pantry's shelves, Ward moved forward . . . and he accidentally stepped on her tail.

I don't think she could have bitten him too hard. I think she was just telling him to watch where he put his feet, but Ward roared fit to part the *Beauty*'s timbers. He kicked my poor little monkey so hard she thumped into the nearest potato sack. Of course she fled, and the quickest way was up. Up the pantry's five shelves she scooted. Ward rubbed his shin, cursing, checking his hand for blood. I couldn't see if he found any. I wasn't hoping that he did. An angry Ward could turn the pantry upside down without any consideration of what might actually conceal a baby. If he tore into the pantry the same way he'd gone after the galley, there was no possibility he wouldn't find Yemaya. There was nothing I could do. Hopelessly, I began to pray.

Allie shouldn't be shaken up when her belly's full. She'd had lunch, she'd had a banana. Now after all that she'd stuffed, and all that shock from

Ward's kick, and all that scooting up five shelves, she turned face forward, leaned over—and lost everything.

It can't have been deliberate.

It *can't* have been deliberate, but where Allie's lunch went was the top of Ward's head. Also his face and his shoulders.

For a moment, Ward froze. Pus-colored broth and undigested banana dripped from his chin and chest. Tiny maggot-like pieces of what might once have been onion all but wriggled on his neck. The lantern's light danced over the pantry as the constable shook with suppressed laughter, his free hand hard over his mouth. Then, in the moment it took the two of us to back away to let Phineas Ward out of the pantry, Allie loosed a second salvo.

I could smell it from the pantry doorway.

Mate's vocabulary is nothing compared to Phineas Ward's.

The two hunters' search ended there. I love Allie, but I have to say that her puke stank even worse than Phineas Ward's hair oil. Proof is that *he* could smell it. He couldn't wait to get off the *Beauty*, back to shore, out of his clothes.

Wordlessly, Portsmouth's constable followed his temporary boss out of the galley. As he passed me, he winked.

I didn't follow. To see them both back in their longboat and headed to shore would have been a joy, but I was sick with a new worry. How soon did I dare lift that top basket? And what was I going to find?

The funny noise I was hearing was my own breathing. Even after all Phineas Ward's shouting, there wasn't a ripple of sound from Yemaya.

As usual after her episodes, Allie was feeling quite subdued. I laid her on a turnip sack and set my shaky hands to disconnecting the false top of Yemaya's basket. Easy, Dr. Spofford had said, to kill somebody by giving him too much laudanum. What if I'd given Yemaya too much?

June 1852

In a place called Boston, they were helped by a skinny white woman with a hat that covered so much of her head, Ogun concluded that she must be bald. She fed them something they'd never had the likes of. Corned beef, she called it, though it was a strange red color unlike any cooked beef Ogun had ever seen, and there wasn't a kernel of corn. Hungry as never before in his life, Ogun swallowed every spoonful without question or comment.

The following night, it was a black man. He'd told them their next stop was a big town called Portland. "Nobody going to take you into town," he'd advised them. "Get there daylight, you wait. Dark come, you wait. Come *almost* daylight, you walk in by your two selfs."

There would be a long, unpainted wooden building atop a hill. The Abyssinian Meeting House, the man had said it was called, but better they should find it without asking anybody. Ogun hadn't needed to be told that.

So many windows on the first floor, so many on the second, the man said, drawing a picture in the dirt with a stick. Two big front doors and a window in between. "You just go in and wait. Somebody come."

"Takes a ship," that somebody had told them when he came, "to get thee where thou'rt going. Come daylight tomorrow, one of us will row thee to a near island and leave thee with some people. They are Friends like us, but the captain of the vessel that stops for thee is not. On that vessel, thou wilt be hidden at once. Now, listen. As soon as the man who hides thee is gone, *hide in a different place.* Hide well. If that man's vessel is stopped and thou art found, he will go to prison, a ruined man. If he sees he's to be searched, thou wilt go over the side before he's even been boarded."

Waiting for a rowboat at Portland's dockside, Ogun's bare toes grip and ungrip the cool cobblestones. His nose isn't offended by the nearby fish market, but he can't stop feeling that the squalling seagulls it attracts are announcing, betraying him.

He wonders if this vessel will be like the one that brought him and his mother from the Pasquotank River to New York City. He tries to remember that one, tries to remember places where two people might hide.

Chapter 17

Flight!

If I had caused Cook's grandchild's death, I would never live long enough to forgive myself, not if I died the oldest man in Massachusetts.

I reminded myself that if I'd given her too little laudanum and she'd wakened and whimpered, she'd have ruined a dozen lives, especially her own, but this reminder didn't stop my hands from shaking as I lifted the top basket.

The little body lay absolutely still, its skin a paler color than I had ever seen it. My heart hit my ribs like a wild pitch. Then the forehead wrinkled in a frown and a tiny thumb searched and found a familiar mouth.

She had *not* whimpered and she had *not* died and she had *not been found*, and Allie was about to become Cook's favorite animal on earth. And I was about to change my pants.

"Cap'n wants you!" Hawk called as I emerged on deck. His message delivered, he didn't pause to see if I obeyed. Mate had the crew flying, preparing the *Beauty* to get underway. The wind seemed to be maybe picking up at last, and Uncle Thad wanted us out of Portsmouth harbor.

He wasn't waiting to find out how we'd got rid of Phineas Ward—who for all he knew might be back! Plus, what if some other bounty hunter had heard the same rumor as Ward?

I agreed that the more sea we put between us and Phineas Ward the better, and leaving Allie behind, I commenced running to the quarterdeck to tell Uncle Thad so. I practically knocked Cook down as he was hurrying to the galley.

"All's well," I gasped, shook off his hands, and ran on.

Uncle Thad was putting his cabin back to rights. Phineas Ward and the constable obviously hadn't wasted any time drinking brandy. From the looks of the cabin, the *Beauty* had weathered a gale. Ward hadn't liked Uncle Thad's attitude. Clearly he'd enjoyed violating Uncle Thad's space while Uncle Thad stood by helpless. I could see that he'd rummaged through places too small for any human alive, like the desk's pen drawer. "Claimed he was looking for *evidence*," said Uncle Thad.

Rubbing it in that he had the whip hand, that's what.

The thing making Uncle Thad maddest was the smashed medicine kit lock. (Three missing laudanum drops weren't noticeable.) "One of 'em must have done it when my back was turned. I couldn't always watch 'em both. All they had to do was ask. I always have the key on me."

I swallowed, sucked in my gut, straightened my shoulders, and told him what I'd done and how it had worked out. "I figured you could get a new lock cheaper than a new schooner."

Uncle Thad sat down. Stared at me. Stood up and shook my hand, shook it hard. Sat down again and laughed till he cried. "Ray, that day you came to me on Bartlett's Wharf was the luckiest day of my life since the day I met your aunt Edith. When that pair of jackals slunk aboard, I thought we were all ruined."

"It was the second-luckiest day of my life too. Sir." (I almost forgot that "sir.") "I guess the luckiest was the day Father gave me Allie."

"And I guess even Cook might agree with you."

Uncle Thad became serious. "Ray, I sent for you because Portsmouth's customs collector had a letter for me from your cousin Ida that I think may interest you."

Cousin Ida's married to a Canadian fisherman, Bert Gray. Grand Manan Island in Canada's Bay of Fundy is their home. "Dear Thad," she'd written, "Bert and our guest and I await you eagerly."

Uncle Thad knew I'd guess this sentence's meaning. That guest was Yemaya's father. But one guest, not three. Yemaya's mother and brother had not arrived.

Yet, I made myself think. Hadn't arrived *yet*.

"You can pass the word," Uncle Thad said.

I knew he wasn't giving me the job of telling Cook just so's to dodge having to relay bad news. Cook didn't normally have business in the captain's cabin, and the last thing we needed after the day's doings was for somebody—Mate—to ask himself why Uncle Thad was sending for Cook just now.

Did Mate believe that Phineas Ward had come on a false tip, or did he think that the *Beauty* had dodged lightning? I prayed it was the former. Guarding that pantry around the clock wasn't easy. Guarding it without arousing suspicion was harder yet, but we would just have to do it. Cook had managed all the way from Charleston, after all, and now he had me to help.

Uncle Thad interrupted my thoughts. "We won't be long at the island. It's not a trade stop; just to drop off our personal delivery to Ida." Normally the next stop the *Beauty* made after Portsmouth was up at Kennebunk, Maine. That plan had been scrapped after I'd reported maybe having seen Phineas Ward at Salisbury, so Cook was already resigned to making do without fresh supplies till we were headed home.

In the meantime, we had plenty of peeled potatoes and chopped garlic.

Back in the galley, Cook and I couldn't have spoken more cautiously to each other about the afternoon's goings on and the change in the *Beauty's* plans. Those gaps in the bulkhead gave anybody in the fo'c'sle access to more from the galley than food smells. They'd hear every word we said. And I still didn't know who besides Hawk was in on Cook and Uncle Thad's secret. And mine.

We sailed up our coast, lines snapping. Our coast. For the first time I was about to venture beyond it, about to look on my first foreign shore. I resolved to start making our crow's nest my post anytime I could escape chores. Allie, since the episode of the stolen bananas, wanted nothing to do with laying aloft. She might sit at the foot of the mast and wear herself out scolding me for choosing the crow's nest over her, but she'd be there when I climbed down.

The morning we sailed past Portland, Maine, Cook was more than a little out of sorts. Getting out of that close pantry, up on the breezy deck, obviously helped him, so I told him just to leave

Yemaya to me. He was feeling bad enough that he agreed. I didn't let on to any anxiety, but when I went to feed her, she hadn't been sucking away for more than a couple of minutes before she up and pushed the cloth knot out of her mouth. Here it comes, I thought, and it was an awful feeling. No way could I get Cook on the scene before Yemaya began to raise the roof. She blinked her eyes open. She saw me, of course; I pretty well filled the scene. Yemaya looked at me and smiled. At me. Well!

The rest of the day's feedings went fine. Allie didn't interfere so long as she was both tied to a barrel and supplied with bananas.

Yemaya took to chirping as I picked her up. When she smiled, she reminded me that she was toothless, and that she had dimples. When Allie smiled, she was reminding me how hard she could bite.

When either one of them gripped my finger with her whole fist, I was surprised to find that the feeling it gave me was very much the same.

Cousin Ida and her husband lived at Dark Harbor, on the west side of Grand Manan. "How about anchoring as far offshore as we can and still make it in by jolly boat?" I suggested to Uncle Thad. "Wouldn't that make Cousin Ida's package seem more casual?"

"You're right, Ray. We will have to anchor off-shore, but as to how far out...the Bay can be rough. We don't want to put that package at risk in a small boat any longer than we must."

"We might have a problem, sir," I ventured. "Mate came on me my first Sunday aboard reading in Hawk's newspaper about William Lloyd Garrison. He swore that any black stowaway he found would find himself swimming in the Atlantic before he could so much as hiccup."

"That strong!" said Uncle Thad. "Heigh-ho. Usually I have a chance to feel a man out before I sign him, but Hiram broke his fool ankle just twenty-four hours before we were due to sail with the first wind. I thought I was lucky to find a hand willing to accept that we'd need him only till Hiram's bone knit. I knew this man's uncle; he was a crony of my father-in-law's." He sighed again. "Once he was aboard, of course, smuggling was the last subject I wanted to bring up. Not to mention the last thing I wanted to attempt till he was gone. But this being Cook's grandchild, we had to take the risk. Can't always choose your times. Well, with any luck, we'll find Hiram ready to come aboard when we put in at Rockport again. But meanwhile . . ."

Uncle Thad let it be known to the crew that because of "the treacherous Bay of Fundy tides," the *Beauty* would anchor well off the coast and send the basket of medical supplies Cousin Ida had requested in by boat. And *I* was to be charged with care of those precious supplies en route. "You weigh considerably less than I do, Ray," Uncle Thad said. "The lighter the load, the easier the rowing. And that is going to be important. Tell Ida I'll write."

At the time, I was pleased with myself.

We had no other business on Grand Manan and would head back toward Portland the minute the jolly boat was aboard again. Had it been a question of turning our backs on a port blessed with plentiful liquor shops and pretty girls, there might have been long faces. As Cousin Ida has complained to Mam, however, "there aren't but about twelve hundred people living on the whole island, and most of them on the far side from us!"

Cook and Uncle Thad were extra careful about how much time Cook was seen conferring in Uncle Thad's quarters, so Uncle Thad, Hawk, and I made careful plans, which I then relayed to Cook for his opinions. What we settled on was this: Hawk and Cook would row. I would mind the double basket. This time instead of greens, the basket top would be filled with the bandages and medicines Uncle Thad had bought in Portsmouth for Cousin Ida's poor little boy who'd hurt his poor little leg falling off a horse.

As I discussed this with Cook, there was a small sound from the pantry. I was closest to the pantry door, and I didn't wait for Cook. Keeping Yemaya quiet was vital for all our sakes. She saw me, and her smile was so big, if Cook hadn't been standing practically beside me by that time, I'd have smiled back.

Then I felt myself smiling anyway. I could swear I heard Cook chuckle, but when my head jerked his way, he had his back turned, heading out the pantry door.

It swung shut behind him. Meanwhile Yemaya was all dimples, so I tickled her chin and fed her. Then I laid her on my shoulder and burped her like a good grandfather, since her real grandfather seemed to be leaving her to me.

Running before the wind in a heavy sea, the *Beauty* rolled. I felt that she shared my impatience to see Grand Manan's dark cliffs. Grand Manan, Canada, where slavery is illegal and our federal government's Fugitive Slave Law is meaningless. I spent as little time cooped up in the galley as I could get away with. It was I, in the crow's nest, who shouted "land ho!"

Up the island's western coast we sailed, mile after mile with never a sight of house or human or the possibility of one. Steep cliffs dark with trees, no welcoming shore. None for the jolly boat and men, anyway.

Dark Harbor's grudging inlet was the first break in the coastline. I needn't have worried. Never could the *Beauty* have sailed through that narrow opening. And for a bonus, neither Mate nor anybody else was going to be able to see who met our jolly boat, or what we gave them.

We would be met, Uncle Thad assured me. "Dark Harbor's no Boston. Our sails will've been noted an hour ago."

The *Beauty* hove to, and the port jolly boat was lowered. From the way it tossed and shipped water, I wondered if two oarsmen would be enough. Allie, I decided, would stay aboard the *Beauty*. Uncle Thad would see her safe back to Father, if it came to that. I didn't explore this thought. I tucked it away as fast as it came.

Today it was Cook who'd put the drop of go-to-sleep in Yemaya's knotted handkerchief. And it was Cook, after Uncle Thad sent Mate below to check a pump, who lowered her basket to Hawk and me in the jolly boat. I stood on my seat to match Hawk's reach, holding my breath. The boat lurched and dipped so, I expected every second to go over the side. Hawk's jaw was clamped as tight as mine. Allie had denounced me for tethering her to the mainmast with Mandy just before I left, but I was glad not to have her on my shoulder at this point! Cook followed the basket down, and the boat rocked again, lapping up even more water, but at least I was sitting down.

Cook picked up the second oar, and we were underway. No big send-off. The Plumers were busy on the sails, carrying out orders Uncle Thad had caused Mate to give them just before Mate went below. Phil Wood had the midnight watch, so he was asleep in his bunk. Uncle Thad waved his spyglass from the quarterdeck.

Then, suddenly, Mate appeared beside him. We were too far to read Mate's expression, but he'd definitely returned much sooner than we expected. Had suspicion hurried him? I suppressed a ridiculous urge to stick my right arm in the water as a third oar.

What, I asked myself, could Mate see, after all? If a head count was what he was after, our little boat passed the test; I grinned.

But what might he find if he went back to investigate the pantry now? Had Cook left something that could get Uncle Thad in trouble? A knotted, milk-dipped rag, a piece of dung too big for a monkey? We'd been awfully careful, Cook and I, to smuggle such things overboard with the regular galley waste. Cooking for eight makes plenty of peelings.

Still, I worried—until a more immediate worry put that one clear out of my mind.

I sat facing our oarsmen. I could see Hawk straining to outrow Cook, and Cook sweating not to let him. Behind them rose Dark Harbor's craggy cliffs. My job was to bail out what wave after wave dumped in on us. I was soon sweating myself, glad that this bending forward hid the fear on my face from the oarsmen.

Our little boat was so tossed and shoved, we were every minute in danger of overturning. With luck, we three could hang on to our capsized boat and pray for a rescue from the *Beauty*, but Yemaya's basket would sink like an anchor. That precious inlet looked farther away than it had looked from on deck, and the waves that challenged us looked too much like the cliffs. Each wave lifted and dropped, lifted and dropped us, I ceasing to breathe each time. And always the smack of our stern back on water was followed by another wave as bad as the last. And then one reared up that was worse.

Chapter 18

Tears

Suddenly I was looking down, not across, at Hawk and Cook. I clutched the seat under me with both arms, Yemaya's basket with both knees. Everything stopped—heartbeat, thought, breath.

We came back down with a slap that jarred my spine.

Another wave like that would sink us. The boat was as helpless as a child in a hammock tormented by bullies. The current was against us. Hawk and

Cook rowed three strokes to move us one stroke's worth. Breathing through their teeth, they kept rowing. And kept rowing.

And God, though not the current, was with us.

The pondlike harbor's still surface was a gift after the rough bay. Now, hidden from the *Beauty*'s view, I could remove the top half of Yemaya's basket. I set the basket on my seat and knelt in the slosh to work on it. Cook evidently didn't have as heavy a hand with the laudanum as I did. Yemaya was beginning to fuss before I got to her.

"Our guest," Cousin Ida had written. I had been praying ever since that a letter written now would say "guests," that Cook's daughter and grandson were waiting for us on that narrow, rocky beach. I was almost afraid to look.

The light was fading, but as we came nearer to shore, I could see a cluster of figures, still as leaf-stripped trees. Three—no, four, the fourth a shrub. My heart began to pound, and as we drew close, the "trees" became a tall, lean black man, an almost equally tall, lean black woman, and my pale, dumpy Cousin Ida. The fourth figure was a boy. On an impulse, I held Yemaya up for all to see.

There was a glad cry from the tall woman, and she rushed into the water to meet us. Her husband splashed in after her. Cook's daughter snatched her child from me and held her close, and we three shipmates waded ashore after them. Hawk and I beached the boat; Cook couldn't wait to embrace his daughter. Only the boy was still, solemn as the angel on my cousin's gravestone. His father was grinning so hard it must have hurt his face; his mother was laughing and crying; Cook was swiping tears off his own beaming face. The boy's eyes remained dry and wide, and I was grateful. I didn't want Hawk to know what a hard time I was having staying dry-eyed, and the boy's stare made it easier.

The next thing I knew, the tall woman was kissing my cheek, her husband was gripping my hand, and the moment he let go, Cousin Ida was hugging me as hard as I've ever been hugged. I was embarrassed, but pleased too.

Cook introduced his grandson to me. "This boy's grandmother name him Ogun," Cook said. "Yoruba blacksmith god Ogun make weapon and make plow. 'This boy will fight his people free,' his grandmother say, 'and then he will feed them.'"

Cook's grandson was skinny and just about as tall as me. He didn't speak or put out his hand, but he looked back at me steadily. I put out my hand, and after a couple of seconds, he took it. Maybe Cook nudged him.

I longed to ask this Ogun a hundred questions: How old are you? How did you get to Grand Manan? How long did it take? What did you eat? Were you ever scared? But Hawk said, "Sorry, folks. Time and tide." Cousin Ida wanted to feed us, and I wouldn't have minded at all. Hawk, though, urged us to make it back aboard the *Beauty* before sunset. And I realized that while joy had put the rough bay clean out of my mind, Hawk had the sense to calculate that should the jolly boat dump us in the water on the way back to the schooner, it would be nice if the men aboard her could see us!

I knew that our return trip would be just as hard, but there was this difference: We were three able-bodied, strong-armed souls who could at least fight the waves, could cling to the overturned boat if it came to that, or try to. None of us was trapped helpless in a seagrass prison. Those were my thoughts as we pushed off. We'd scarcely passed out of the inlet into the bay when my mood lurched.

I was the one who saw it first, a dark triangle rising at least two feet out of the water and coming steadily toward us. "What's that?" I cried, but I knew.

June 1852

From the night he heard the cabin door close behind his father for the last time, life has been questions for Ogun. That message from his father that set his mother and himself on their road north answered the most important one, but none of the others has been small. Will his father leave him and his mother again? If he does, how will Ogun take care of the two of them in this strange hilly, foggy place, this place with no steady rivers but a world of bullying ocean? Take care, that is, of the two of them and now that baby.

That baby has been given a second name since Ogun's grandfather brought her back; she has become Yemaya Yewande. Yemaya is a goddess, Ogun's mother told him a long time ago, still on the plantation. That baby doesn't look anything like a goddess. *Yewande* means "Mother has returned" in Yoruba, Ogun's mother says. That baby is learning to smile at

Ogun, and Ogun is learning to call that baby Yemaya Yewande for serious exchanges, Yummy for short ones.

Ogun has heard his parents planning. They won't stay on this island; there's no work, his father says. They will go to a place called Novaskosha. Who will feed them there? Where will they sleep? Ogun's father seems to think he can take care of all that. Ogun is glad he brought his slingshot.

Ogun watches this grandfather of his get into that small boat with the white boy and the man with eyebrows like the hawk Ogun used to see stealing eagles' fish. He wonders if he will ever see this grandfather again. He wonders if his mother will tell him now who took Yummy from her cradle and how this grandfather got her. Could that white boy have been the one who came and took her? There were a hundred questions Ogun wanted to ask that boy. How old is he? How did he hide Yemaya Yewande? Did Ogun's grandfather pay him to do it?

Was he ever scared?

Chapter 19

The Devil's Wind

A shark can smell a meal half a mile away, Father says. *This one must have smelled us on our trip in and come too late to catch us,* I figured. So it had waited. My whole body shrank.

I have been scared of sharks for as long as I can remember. My bedroom rug is blue as the sea on a cloudless day, and when I was young, I was so scared of sharks I could only get to sleep in the very middle of my bed.

Now I clenched my teeth. "Never let fear be your captain," says Father. "Stay the master of your own ship, whatever." What nonsense, I mocked myself, to imagine a shark lying in wait for our return trip. What reason would it have had to expect our return? Then I saw that there were two fins, the smaller following the larger by several feet only. The big shark's mate, I guessed. The hair on my arms stood up so straight it pulled.

Cook and Hawk had twisted around at my cry. Now they turned back to face me, but though those fins continued to bear down on us, neither man resumed rowing. Stock-still they sat, jaws rigid. Scared helpless? Or, worse, resigned? Either thought shocked me cold.

"Be real quiet," Hawk murmured. "Don't alarm him. He'll swamp us if he thrashes this close. If he breaches, we're gone." He, not they: The creature was now so close I could see that what I'd mistaken for a mate's dorsal fin was the one shark's tail. I was too frightened to feel foolish. I sat like Cook and Hawk, still as a gravestone, willing my heart to beat quietly.

The shark was easily twice the length of our

boat. Its ugly, swollen, funnel-shaped snout stuck up just above the water, and as it came abreast of us, we could see the rest of the great gray body clearly. The wide-open mouth was big enough to take a hog in one gulp. And me in two? Beside us the shark rolled slightly, sized us up with one little unblinking piggy eye—and kept swimming.

I have never minded being rejected less.

"Basking shark," pronounced Hawk calmly while our boat was still rocking in the monster's wake. "Them kind don't bite. But that'n'll weigh in at seven ton easy. You don't want to get him excited anywhere near your boat! Turn us over in a fart."

Now I noticed that the water around us was hazy with what looked like sieved spinach. This was what our shark was feeding on, straining it out of the water through hundreds of tiny teeth as it swam with its cave-size mouth wide open.

"Ugly," said Cook. I wondered if that mouth made him think of the *Beauty*'s crew at chow time.

"He had me thinkin' 'Tell my mother I loved her' for a while there," said Hawk. "When a basker takes a notion to breach—well, I've seen one eye to eye, and me standin' on the quarterdeck! Glad this one was by himself. When the feed was good, I've seen 'em a dozen at a time." He and Cook resumed rowing.

Who knew "this one" wouldn't turn and come again? Bring his friends? Calculating the chances of our not being spilled by a pod a dozen strong made me weak. Bailing was a welcome distraction from constantly estimating the distance between us and the *Beauty*.

The wind was so strong that this distance almost seemed to be a constant. The very wind that we would bless if ever we got back aboard the *Beauty* seemed to be making sure we never would. Cook sweated, and Hawk grunted, and I felt bad about the weight I was adding without being able to help. I bent over double bailing, so I wouldn't have to see a look on their faces that said they regretted the same thing. If I'd had on shoes, I'd have thrown them overboard, just to lighten the load by that much.

At last Cook had to take a breather. Now the wind actually moved us farther away from the *Beauty*. I half rose to take Cook's oar, but Hawk shook his head, and Cook, scowling, bent his back again. By the time we fetched up beside the *Beauty*, I was surprised either oarsman had the strength left to climb aboard.

My welcome was a scolding from Allie.

Mate had less to say, but from the suspicious way he looked at us, I was powerful glad we'd left Yemaya's basket behind with her. We downright did not need Mate sniffing around the galley, inspecting that fake-bottomed basket.

"All hands!" Mate bellowed. "Heave up anchor!"

We sailed with all sails set. As we left the Bay, the lighthouse on Machias Seal Island seemed to bless us.

I felt wistful. There'd be no welcoming family for *me* when we moored again at Newburyport, with Father at sea and Mam in Boston. Somehow I didn't expect Uncle Slye to hurry down to the wharves and beg Allie and me to come back. The picture of him on his knees imploring returned a smile to my face—the first favor Uncle Slye ever did me.

Seeing Cook embrace his family had made me homesick for my parents, but I knew I was going to see them again sometime. Cook didn't know that about his daughter and her children. They were headed for Nova Scotia, where her husband knew some other men who'd made it to freedom. Cook, though, set his jaw. He complained only that we were out of fresh meat.

If Cook and I are lucky, his daughter will find some way to send a message back to Cousin Ida about how she makes out in Nova Scotia. Cousin Ida will write Uncle Thad, and Uncle Thad will tell Cook and me. But I wish I were going to be around to see Yemaya's face when she takes her first steps. She has a smile that will light up a whole house—if she's let out of the pantry.

Cook's desire for the next port's provisioning took a hit during the night. The wind died. Climbing up out of the fo'c'sle hatch at seven bells was like poking my head into wet cotton. Fog. I felt my way to the galley. The ladder down to the main deck felt damp to the soles of my feet; the galley door was damp to my hand. Inside, Cook had lit a lantern against the gloom.

We could see no better through the fog after the

sun rose, but I could hear our limp sails flapping. We were becalmed.

A Newburyport Fourth of July is bigger than anything but Christmas, and I'd begun trying to tell Allie about it, thinking we'd surely be back in time. I could tell she didn't understand at all, and now I thought that was just as well. As hour after dreary hour passed, I began to brood. We all knew stories of ships becalmed so long they ran out of food and water. And of what their crews did then. First, of course, we would eat poor Mandy. Then we'd draw straws. Unless Allie and I, being the least useful, would go next without further formalities.

Thoughts like this were ridiculous on day one, I reproved myself, and I tried to come up with something to keep them at bay. Name our presidents, Washington to Fillmore. Name the thirty-one states. Work through the multiplication table. Time was a crippled snail. On the fo'c'sle deck, Mate strode back and forth whistling tunelessly between muttered curses. When he threw a penny into the waves, the crew exchanged looks. "Bad luck," Cook told me. "Man whistle for wind, buy wind from devil, never get to say how *much* wind." Dinner in the fo'c'sle was eaten in silence.

But everyone was more cheerful when the fog lifted midway through the afternoon and a freshening breeze filled our sails.

This cheerfulness was temporary. We had yet to glimpse the Maine coast when silent lightning to our north set the crew, including Cook, to taking in all sail. Even Mate lent a hand. A storm doesn't ask your rank when it tatters your sails and leaves you drifting to starvation.

No more does it ask for what slot you signed on. As soon as I could hustle Mandy below to her nighttime/bad weather pen and tether Allie to one of its posts, I hurried back to help with the sails. Allie scolded—if anything, worse than the day before. I didn't take time to explain to her, which I guess was a mistake.

The sharp smell that greeted me back on deck reminded me of when Tom Chase and I douse our campfire with river water. *Lightning.* And the wind Mate had bargained for seemed to be planning to mention who was boss. Good that I knew where to lay a hand, for nobody had time to tell me. Hawk and Phil had eyes only for their work. Jim and Tim darted every other glance at the massing clouds. Thunder rumbled and lightning spider-webbed the sky.

We were squared away none too soon. Great balls of light danced, now at the masthead, now at the yardarms, now red, now blue, and the rain came like a dam burst. For a full minute, I couldn't see another soul, though I knew myself surrounded. The *Beauty* tossed and pitched so violently, waves ran over the decks shin deep. "If you see a ship-sized sea a-comin' at you, lad, make for the rigging!" Father had taught me, but who could tell what the waves looked like, or where the rigging was for that matter? The rain was blinding. But when I gasped, once, the water that instantly filled my mouth was salty.

Anything loose—a bucket, a coil of rope, a carelessly stowed jolly boat oar—was carried, now to our port side, now starboard, now aft, now straight for the bow. I was nearly knocked off my feet by something I never did identify. Had I lost my footing, I knew how fast I'd have been swept overboard.

Under our feet, the deck trembled. Then as we groped our way toward the fo'c'sle deck ladder, a quick succession of lightning flashes showed me Allie, helpless in the rushing water. Free of my hasty tying, she had made her way to the deck.

I lunged for her.

A bony hand gripped my shoulder, jerking me back. Through the not-quite-solid rain I caught a glimpse of black whiskers and guessed that the hand holding me fast and the voice making itself heard above the storm were Tim Plumer's.

"Ye can't help 'er! Ye'll go over yerself!"

Chapter 20

Allie Too

People who say a thing can't be done should keep out of the way of people doing that thing.

I wrenched free and plunged after Allie as the *Beauty* dipped and a great wave carried us both straight toward the bow. I didn't even have time to pray, but by God's mercy I grasped Allie and the foremast stopped me. Together we were pinned fast. Though we were helpless to move ourselves, I knew the water would carry us the other way any moment. Allie clung to me while with my free hand I grabbled about and found a rope to hold on to when the great water rushed aft. Not to be rushed with it took nearly all my strength. I had just enough left to breathe three grateful times, then to pull myself to my feet.

Now the sea seemed to have been wakened by the rain, and the poor *Beauty* dipped and reared like a demon-possessed sled. No sooner was she down one hill than she rushed straight up the next even faster, and down and up and down and up, with never a breath between, every timber creaking so, I dreaded the *Beauty* would fly apart, hurling every one of us into the infinite stew. Allie held me fast as I groped with both hands, inching our way to shelter. I chose the galley door rather than the ladder my mates were struggling up. I didn't have the strength left to climb. Allie and I fell in a heap on the galley floor.

Cook had beaten us there. He crawled over, and in a frenzy of indignation (this storm was Mate's fault—his reckless whistling, his penny!), he rubbed Allie dry with dish towels. Me he ordered out of my sopping shirt and trousers, no wetter than his own. Given how the *Beauty* was tossing, obeying wasn't easy. It was a long time before I was wrapped in one of his sheets, he in another, and we were all three drinking hot milk sweetened with molasses, but when that time came, I believe Cook was as grateful as I that Mandy was on a two-good-milkings-a-day schedule now.

By evening, nothing remained of Mate's storm but the great blue bruise on my thigh where I'd fetched up against the foremast and a deck so slickery I nearly fell, heading below to give Mandy hay for the night.

I winced to catch myself blaming Mate for our storm like the most superstitious sailor afloat. Now that he was no threat, I was going over everything in my mind, ashamed that I'd suspected him of trying to drown me, wondering if some of my worries about him and Yemaya had been half-cocked. But I decided not. Mate was so worried about his own hide, he'd have done just what he said, chucked anybody overboard who he thought was a threat to his own freedom. It would be a good day when he stepped ashore in Rockport and Hiram came back. Mate, I was sure, was thinking the same thing himself.

I did feel sheepish about suspecting Mate of trying to lose me off the bowsprit. What would it have gained him? Talk about half-cocked. But clearly the man resented my having a boyhood so much smoother than his own. I compromised with myself: He hadn't been trying to drown me, just test me—but he wouldn't have burst into great salt tears if I'd drowned on my own.

Cook and I served squash pies for supper. Allie seemed happy to share mine. I wanted to ask her if stolen pies were sweeter, but not in Cook's hearing. Allie was still testing her tail when she thought nobody was looking. It gripped perfectly, of course, but she was staying off masts. And she wasn't stealing pies.

As for all the others, they were glad to have got through all those potatoes I'd peeled at Portsmouth.

From Portland to Kennebunk, we had fair winds. The days seemed strange, though, without Yemaya in the pantry. I didn't have to remind myself that it was good, of course, that she was with her mother.

Maybe all I really missed was hearing that banjo in the pantry off and on.

Truthfully, I guess not.

The crew was cheerful. I suspected the men were counting the days till the *Beauty* docked at Rockport and Hiram Upham came back to his old post . . . and Mate left her decks for good. My suspicions doubled when I saw that Jim Plumer was letting his beard grow again.

But I was not destined still to be aboard the *Beauty* when she docked at Rockport.

At Salisbury, the customs collector had a letter for Uncle Thad from Father—sent from Newburyport! Both my parents were back.

Father's homecomings always meant exciting stories, but this time my feelings were mixed. Uncle Thad had agreed that Allie and I would just have to stay on his schooner for another voyage if Mam wasn't home from Boston. I'd looked forward to that. Now instead I was practicing my excuse for having run away and boarded the *Beauty* when I was supposed to be working for Uncle Slye. "Don't come back till you're rid of that monkey!" Uncle Slye'd told me. So I was just obeying when I didn't go back. That was the line I was working on, but it was going to take some more work because that wasn't really exactly what he'd said. (I couldn't claim it was Uncle Slye's treachery to Uncle Thad that had set my feet moving, because I hadn't yet grasped that at the time. Plus, it was not a story for dockside telling!)

A few hours after we sailed out of Salisbury, I saw something that changed my attitude completely regarding leaving the *Beauty*. From the moment I saw it, I couldn't get Allie off the schooner fast enough: Allie had learned to milk Mandy. And she didn't use a pail.

Newburyport at last! Lugging my stuffed bag, Allie on my shoulder, I climbed up through the fo'c'sle hatch. The alongshoremen were unloading the *Beauty*'s hold already. I spied my parents at once, standing beside Uncle Thad. I felt both eager and apprehensive; I rehearsed my story once more.

Cook was waiting for me at the foremast. We shook hands good-bye and then he was hugging me, to Allie's astonishment and mine.

"Boy," he said, "you been a Ray of sunshine, a Ray of hope." He thrust a small sack into my hand.

For an instant, I was startled. Then I felt so proud I was ashamed of myself.

Maybe I'll never again feel exactly the same way about our cheek-bruising minister's wife as I used to.

Maybe my cheek is tougher, now that I've been to sea.

I didn't come down to earth and look in Cook's sack till I got almost to the gangplank. One dozen buns, brown as mushrooms and just as light.

And at the end of the plank, my parents.

When my gang had stopped by the house to see if I was there again, Mam and Father'd promised a quarter to the first one who brought them news that the *Newburyport Beauty* had been sighted. I was glad when Mam said it was Tom Chase who got the quarter.

Hawk, heading home for a short but appreciated visit, stopped to shake hands with my father. And to clap me on the back and say, "This is a boy who knows how to keep his mouth shut!"

I'd give a quarter myself for the look on Mam's face.

Hawk didn't know the half of it, I thought. I squeezed Allie the milker's guilty paw.

As I'd stepped off the gangplank, Father'd thrown an arm around me. Judging by which of his buttons had nearly hit my eye, I was almost certain that sea air really had made me grow. (Dr. Spofford *says* it does.) But when I mentioned this to Father, he laughed.

"Your uncle's already told me you're nine feet tall, Ray." His left hand came out from behind him, and he slapped a sailor's wide-brimmed, red-ribboned hat on my head.

I'd wondered why his welcoming hug had been one-armed!

"Try wearing this the next time you stand under that mantelpiece," Father said. "If it doesn't do the trick, we'll lower the mantel. How would you like to see Cádiz?"

I stared at him. Then I looked at Mam. Mam turned both hands palm upward and managed a smile.

I smiled at Father. "Allie too?" The *Black Skimmer* doesn't have a goat.

"Allie too. Unless your mother insists on keeping her."

Allie too.

ACKNOWLEDGMENTS

My father's first American grandsire, Aquila Chase, is honored by historians of European, rather than Algonquian, descent as the first man to pilot a vessel across the bar at the mouth of the Merrimack River. Certainly he was the first of either background to maintain a ferry on the Merrimack. In 1646, he moved from Hampton, New Hampshire, to Newburyport, Massachusetts, to avoid a second fine for "picking pease on the Sabbath." He declared that, as a six-day-a-week ferryboat pilot and faithful Sunday-morning churchgoer, he had no opportunity to garden but Sunday afternoons, and he moved across the river. He was grateful that Newburyport was sympathetic to his vegetables' needs, and so am I.

I am indebted to the Kentucky Arts Council for their support in the past.

The books and pamphlets called to my attention, borrowed for me, and given and lent to me by archivists and librarians were indispensable, as were their painstaking replies to my many queries. Particularly helpful were librarians Lynn Buckley Aber, Joseph P. Copley Research Library, Portsmouth Athenæum, and Nicole Luongo Cloutier, Special Collection, Portsmouth Public Library, Portsmouth, NH; Mark Adler, Susan Eads, and Mona Proctor, Paris–Bourbon County Public Library, Paris, KY; Maria Bernier and Wendy Schnur, Mystic Seaport, Museum of America and the Sea, Mystic, CT; Judy Besancon, Newburyport Archives, and Jessica Gill, Newburyport Public Library, Newburyport, MA; William Biles, Matthew Gilley, Carol Moore, Denise Shanks, and Jim Witham, Lexington Public Library, Lexington, KY; Kate Boyd, the South Carolina Room, Charleston County Public Library, Charleston, SC; Bruce Boylen, California State University Maritime Library, Vallejo, CA; William Garvin, Drury University; Josh Graml, The Mariners' Museum, Newport News, VA; Harry McKown, North Carolina Collection, University of North Carolina at Chapel Hill; and Britta Karlberg, Phillips Library, Peabody Essex Museum, Salem, MA.

Some people without whose special professional knowledge I could not have written this book are Anne Beazley, Columbia, SC's Riverbanks Zoo and Garden volunteer worker; Pat Lowery Collins, author of *Schooner*; Burgin E. Dossett III, architect and ship builder; Frances and Herman Finkbeiner, sailors; Robert Garvin, USN ret.; Michael Horne, pharmacist; Susian Lambert of the Grand Manan Tourism Bureau; Drs. Karl and Kathryn Schroeder; and chefs David Buehler and C. O. Trussell.

I owe particular thanks to Karen Leet, without whose advice I do not think this book would have found a publisher. I am grateful for suggestions from Dr. Stephanie Bailey, Debbie Baird, and Beth Gawlik, who read selections from the manuscript, and for the eagle eye of the University of Kentucky's Professor Harry LeVine, who read nearly the whole thing and offered golden advice at uncounted leaden spots. Thanks to Benjamin Leal and Diana Trussell for saving me from computer-generated hysteria time after time; to my sisters Katherine Mears and Anne Robins, who augmented my memory and understanding of our late father's tales of the USS *Delaware*'s monkey; to my brother George T. Wells, USAF, ret., for assisting me with nautical matters and with techniques of survival in marsh and forests, including monkey catching; to my Up Country South Carolina great-grandmother, for all the Buh Rabbit stories she taught my mother; and to writer and sailor Cynthia King for her repeated close readings of early manuscript drafts and informed, meticulous, professional criticism.

My special thanks to Kentucky bookstores like Fort

Thomas's Blue Marble and Lexington's Joseph-Beth Booksellers and the Morris Book Shop, who are so generously supportive of local talent. I am enormously grateful to Ana Deboo for her astonishing vigilance, to Jennifer Weltz and Jessica Regel for their patient and valuable counsel, and to the meticulous Noa Wheeler for getting more out of me than was there.

Most of all to my late husband, Martin, without whom nothing.

GLOSSARY

aft—Toward, near, or in the rear.

alongshoremen—Men who work along the shore, loading and unloading vessels at seaport wharves, for example. Nowadays generally rendered "longshoremen."

beam—The widest part of a boat.

boom—A horizontal spar attached to the bottom edge of a sail to extend it, riding on the mast.

bowsprit—A spar running out from the vessel's bow, the forward part of a vessel, to which are fastened strong ropes from the foremast.

bulkhead—An upright partition separating compartments on a vessel.

bulwarks—The sides of a vessel's uppermost deck, which protect people and objects from going overboard.

capstan—A large, spool-shaped winch with rope or cable wound around it that is used for hauling up sails or anchors.

chafing gear—A covering (usually sheepskin, rope, or canvas) on a line or spar to protect it from friction.

clipper—A fast, square-rigged ship with at least three masts.

crow's nest—A protected lookout position high on the foremast.

dead ahead—Directly ahead.

fo'c'sle (forecastle)—The space beneath the deck forward of the foremast. Also often used to mean the deck itself.

fo'c'sle deck (forecastle deck)—The deck forward of the foremast, above the forecastle.

fore-and-aft—Lengthwise, running from stem to stern, parallel to a vessel's keel. For example, a schooner is fore-and-aft rigged, which makes the sails often appear to run parallel to her sides.

foremast—Mast closest to stem.

foremast stays—Strong ropes from the foremast to the bowsprit.

gaff—A free-swinging spar attached to the top of a schooner's gaffsail.

gaffsail—A four-sided sail secured to the gaff at the top and at its forward edge to a mast.

galley—A vessel's kitchen.

gangplank—A long, narrow, movable platform used for entering or leaving a vessel.

hatch—An opening in the deck of a vessel, usually covered.

head—Toilet space.

headrail—A curved rail at the front of a ship, extending from the place of the figurehead to the bow.

hold—Cargo space belowdecks.

jib—A triangular sail set upon a stay or its own luff, extending from the head of the foremast to the bowsprit.

jolly boat—A medium-size boat used for rough work.

keel—A vessel's backbone, forming her bottom centerline.

lay aloft—Climb.

luff—The forward edge of a fore-and-aft sail.

mainmast—The second mast on a multimasted schooner.

mast—A long pole rising from a vessel's keel through any decks and into the air to sustain yards, booms, sails, and rigging generally.

mate—The second-in-command on a merchant vessel.

mizzenmast—The third mast from the stem.

oakum—Loose fiber obtained by untwisting and picking old hemp ropes, used especially for caulking ship seams. Oakum is tarred, pounded into the seams, painted, and puttied in an effort to keep a vessel watertight.

packet—A vessel having fixed sailing days for carrying mail, passengers, and goods, which in the case of the *Elizabeth Fry* were fruits and vegetables grown by local Quaker farmers.

port—The left side of the vessel when facing forward.

quarterdeck—The raised deck between the mainmast and the boat's rear end, or stern.

ratlines—Small ropes.

reef—To take in part of a sail in order to decrease the area of canvas. Also, the part of the sail taken in by reefing.

rigging—A collective term for equipment, including masts, spars, sails, shrouds, and stays.

schooner—A fore-and-aft-rigged vessel with two or more masts and gaffsails.

ship—A large, oceangoing, square-rigged vessel with three or more masts.

spar—A pole on a vessel, such as a mast, boom, gaff, or yard.

square-rigged—Having the principal sails extended on yards suspended horizontally at the middle.

starboard—The right side of the vessel when facing forward.

stem—The structural upright timber at a vessel's bow.

stern—The rear end of a vessel or boat.

windlass—A heavy mechanical device that pulls cable or chain to raise and lower sails and anchors, hoist cargo in and out of the hold, and "trim" the sail—swing it to and fro to catch as much wind as possible.

yard—A spar usually fixed horizontally to a mast to support a square sail. The yardarm is either end of a square-rigged vessel's yard.

GOFISH

MARTHA BENNETT STILES

What did you want to be when you grew up?
I wanted to be a boy, and I didn't want to wait till I grew up, either. Unable to reach my elbow to kiss it (such a kiss being reputed to turn one instantly into a boy), I vowed I would break my arm and *then* I could turn into a boy. Luckily my older sister told me that wouldn't count—the arm had to be unaltered. This news did not sit well.

When did you realize you wanted to be a writer?
As a schoolgirl.

What's your most embarrassing childhood memory?
The first embarrassment I remember occurred when I was three. When I was waiting to get my tonsils removed, two or three attractive young men came to roll me into the operating room and I was told to transfer myself from my bed to their cart. I didn't comply because I was embarrassed to be wearing only a nightgown. The chaps concluded that I didn't recognize them in their masks and was frightened; they laughed and lowered their masks so I could see they were safe. I, figuratively speaking, shook my head over their foolishness—of course I recognized them. But I resigned myself to complying, as it would have been just as embarrassing to explain my reluctance.

What's your favorite childhood memory?
One blissful memory is of visiting distant cousins in Shepherds-town, West Virginia, when I was six. They had chandeliers. They had a hammock beside a goldfish pond around which autumn crocus—entirely new to me—were blooming. They had a Della Robbia nativity cemented into the wall in their calving stall. They had a bowlful of sugar lumps on their sideboard at all times and didn't mind how many my sister and I ate. (Fortunately my mother took a stand on this.)

As a young person, whom did you look up to most?
Perhaps my grandfather, John Bennett, a writer. I loved him dearly.

What was your favorite thing about school?
Glee club.

What was your first job, and what was your "worst" job?
My first out-in-the-world job was as a telephone operator. My worst job was having, as a high school student, to kill a new-born kid (because the goat was a buck, and we needed its mother's milk). I do not forgive my father for that assignment.

What book is on your night stand now?
Tracy Barrett's splendid *King of Ithaka*.

How did you celebrate publishing your first book?
I celebrated when the book was accepted by the publisher. Given the news, I telephoned my husband at his chemistry lab. When he got home he was carrying a laboratory bucket full of ice plus a bottle of champagne. I telephoned two of our dearest friends and said to the wife, "I've got three drumsticks and a

bottle of champagne." She replied, "I've got three pork chops and we're coming over."

Where do you write your books?
At my desk, in my office.

What sparked your imagination for *Sailing to Freedom*?
An anecdote of my father—who was a naval officer—about a pie-stealing pet monkey on one of the ships of his youth.

What type of research did you do for *Sailing to Freedom*?
It helped that I had already been to Newburyport, Massachusetts (the second book I published was *The Strange House at Newburyport*, about the Underground Railroad), and I had been many times to South Carolina, my mother's native state. I read dozens of books and articles about Newburyport, schooners, capuchin monkeys, the Fugitive Slave Law, rice plantations, slavery, mid-nineteenth-century clothing, schooling, medicine, and so on.

What challenges do you face in the writing process, and how do you overcome them?
"Resist the vision!" cried Michigan's most famous poet, Ted Roethke. A scene occurs to me so vividly, dialogue and all, that I rush to the chase. Facts, like when certain things happened, might make my plot impossible. The most remarkable contortions are required to keep my vivid scene and still have my story possible. (Sometimes I have to give my characters amnesia, things like that.)

Which of your characters is most like you?
Sarah from *Sarah the Dragon Lady*, but she's smarter. Kate from *Kate of Still Waters*, but she's braver. Ruth Brough from

Lonesome Road is like me in her passionate feelings about children, but unlike me in her casual attitude to studies.

What makes you laugh out loud?
The last time I laughed out loud was at a performance of *You Ain't Nothin' but a Hound Dog* during the University of Kentucky's music department's "A Grand Night For Singing." The man playing the worthless wretch could make any part of his body go limp; his lady fair was pure outrage. They were magnificent.

What do you do on a rainy day?
Read and write.

What's your idea of fun?
Reading, writing, stimulating conversation, listening to music, eating well. A good movie, whether on TV or in a theater. My eyes are no longer good enough for tennis—I don't know which of two balls to swat at. I grew up on a river and especially liked swimming underwater—still prefer it. As for horseback riding, I've always had to pretend it was fun and that I wasn't scared or uncomfortable or both.

What's your favorite song?
There's a duet in the opera *The Pearl Fishers* that always captures me. I made the mistake of reading the translated words once and have taken care to forget them; there was nothing sublime about them. But the music is sublime.

Who is your favorite fictional character?
Among those of my own creation, maybe Ogun. He is quietly brave, thoughtful, looking ahead, taking on responsibilities that would flatten many a grown man. And me.

What was your favorite book when you were a kid?
One that I read repeatedly was *The Sword in the Stone.*

Do you have a favorite book now?
No, I am too much like poet Robert Browning's "last duchess," who "liked whate'er she looked on, and her looks went everywhere."

What's your favorite TV show or movie?
Starting at six, I went to *Snow White* three times, and I guess that's enough. On TV, I stop and watch *The Godfather* any time I happen upon it.

If you were stranded on a desert island, whom would you want for company?
Professor Martin Stiles.

If you could travel anywhere in the world, where would you go and what would you do?
Dieppe, France, and do research for a book I have begun about her Huguenots.

If you could travel in time, where would you go and what would you do?
I would go back to the day I graduated from college and do everything sensibly from that moment on.

What's the best advice you have ever received about writing?
Cut.

What advice do you wish someone had given you when you were younger?
Ask more questions.

Do you ever get writer's block? What do you do to get back on track?

The closest I have come to writer's block was putting my work toward my book *The Star in the Forest* away and forbidding myself to look at it for one calendar year. But I wrote other things steadily all that year.

What do you want readers to remember about your books?

I hope they are interesting.

What would you do if you ever stopped writing?

Read. And probably eat too much.

What do you wish you could do better?

Write.

What would your readers be most surprised to learn about you?

I'm not about to tell you.